ed subject to the Ru'
not later than th

Kenneth J. Harvey

Inside

Harvill *Secker*

LONDON

Published by Harvill Secker, 2006

2 4 6 8 10 9 7 5 3 1

First published in Great Britain in 2006 by
HARVILL SECKER
Random House, 20 Vauxhall Bridge Road
London SW1V 2SA

Random House Australia (Pty) Limited
20 Alfred Street, Milsons Point, Sydney,
New South Wales 2061, Australia

Random House New Zealand Limited
18 Poland Road, Glenfield,
Auckland 10, New Zealand

Random House (Pty) Limited
Isle of Houghton, Corner of Boundary Road & Carse O'Gowrie,
Houghton 2198, South Africa

The Random House Group Limited Reg. No. 954009
www.randomhouse.co.uk

A CIP catalogue record for this book is available from the British Library

ISBN 9780436205934 (hardback – from Jan. 07)
ISBN 0436205939 (hardback)
ISBN 9781846550263 (trade paperback – from Jan. 07)
ISBN 1846550262 (trade paperback)

Papers used by Random House are natural, recyclable products made
from wood grown in sustainable forests; the manufacturing processes conform
to the environmental regulations of the country of origin

Typeset in Sabon by
Palimpsest Book Production Limited, Polmont, Stirlingshire
Printed and bound in Great Britain by
Clays Ltd, St Ives plc

For John

Chapter One

They had made a mistake. They had realized. Everything he had moved through. The trail behind him. The institutional walls that kept him. The day in and day out. The tangle of men. It was meant to go away.

Each step he took from his cell to the admitting office was fixed in his memory. Years of what was there and what wasn't. If the thought came to him. He'd shut it off. The things that were missing.

He tried not to feel himself moving. Tightened up against each action. Refused to see the eyes set steady on him. Being led toward 9 a.m.. Release.

He had sat in the same admitting office fourteen years ago. He had taken in every detail then. Went spitefully through the process. Money and valuables removed. Receipt signed by him. File started. Name. Address. Next of kin. Religion. Offense. Photo taken. Strip search. Shower in the stall across the way. Clothes returned to him. Cell assigned. His mind troubled by the process for months after. Picking it over, again and again. Impossible to make different.

Now, he was in that room again.

The sheriff handed him the receiver.

'Hello,' he said. The feel of the phone in his hand was something he did not like.

'Hi, Poppy. I see you on TV all the time. You're famous. You're coming home, right? I can't wait to see you.'

Her little voice. Tears blurred the floor where he was looking.

He said few words because words were hard for him after all this time. Then he hung up.

The sheriff gave him his belongings and, with a bowed head, said: 'This way.'

He left the admitting office. Saw the shower stall across the corridor. He should be made to take one now. Before they let him out. Clean him off. Scour him. But it didn't happen. Only what came in mattered.

He followed the uniform through the locked door and across the yard. The high walls topped with coils of barbed wire. The towers with guards in them when he first came in. No guards there now. Video cameras everywhere. Nothing moving in that yard. Just the two of them. Him and the uniform. He looked back at the windows. The faces there watching him go. Time dead in their eyes.

Up ahead, there was a female guard. On a wooden walkway behind a tall wire fence. She unlocked the gate to let them pass alongside the visiting area. Like a school portable when he was young. Then through another locked gate. Keys rattling. Through another door. Not made of steel or wire. A room made of wood instead of cinder block. The sound of it underfoot. Different air. Different mood. Almost normal. Easy. People waiting to visit. Ordinary people who could come and go. Outside life written all over them. The metal detector. Passing through. Thinking he might set it off for no good reason. The video camera showing the other side of the main door. The crowd gathered there in the parking lot. Moving around but silent on that screen. Waiting for his release. He saw the book for signing in and out. Resting on a ledge. The different signatures. He passed by the visitors. They watched him move. Like they had never seen a man move before. He listened carefully. Edgy. Waiting to hear the buzz of the main door. He thought it might not come. The weight in his chest. His breathing. His shoulders aching. Trying not to show anything. Just another day. One exactly like all the others.

'They're here about you,' the sheriff smiled toward the door.

The female guard was there. Just as the door buzzed. A hand on a button somewhere in the pen. That's how it always happened. Fingers on buttons somewhere you did not see. Doors buzzing. The female guard leaned and pushed open the metal door. He would not look at her. She was smiling a little. Trying to mean business but be nice.

Everything came in. Everything went out. That one door opened to the outside. No handcuffs. Fresh air. Fresh noise and movement that hurt his ears and eyes. Everyone turned to face him. Came toward him. Almost rushed. No restraints. His body filled with warning. Muscles stiffening. His bundle of belongings tucked tighter under his arm. His big hands dangled by his sides. People in the crowd spoke his name right away. They called him Mister Myrden. All of them calling that name out. There were cameras and microphones. Just as there had been before he went in. Some of the same people. Standing there with changed faces. Everything else the same. The need in them still rabid.

The air was cold. There was wind out here. No walls for it to run up against. It stung his skin. He felt it in his hair. In his scalp. In his fingertips so they pulsed to his heartbeat. The landscape beyond the crowd stretched away. Farther and farther. Such endless height and distance. Dizziness in his head and stomach.

'Mister Myrden. Mister Myrden . . .'

His name again and again. And the push of them blocking his way so it was difficult for him to get through.

*

He was driven to his wife's house by his son, Danny. Nineteen years old. The second youngest of five boys and one girl. The house belonged to someone else. He had no idea who. He never asked. He only knew that his wife lived there now.

He sat in the back because the front was too much for him. The big window. The movement of everything at once. It pained his eyes. He thought he might throw up. He watched out the door window in a daze. A smaller piece of glass. The view sharp and confined, framed there. And it kept going along. So many people outside. Moving around as they pleased. Nothing was stopping him. Holding him back. Preventing him.

The car slowed at a set of lights. A thin woman in a coat walked by. Glanced in at him. Nothing to hold her eyes there. Just another man sitting in a car. She kept going. Walking. Her legs a blur. He shut his eyes. He feared that it might be wrong. Opening his eyes, he looked over his shoulder. They were moving again. Cars and vans following him. The people in there all wanted to know what he thought. How does it feel to be a free man? What are your plans? Who really killed Doreen Stagg? Mister Myrden. Freedom. Plans. He watched toward his son. He saw Danny's hand on the steering wheel, the tattooed words on his fingers.

'Those fuckers,' said Danny. 'How fucking angry does

that make you?' Danny's eyes in the rearview. Getting meaner. 'You gonna kick the shit outta Grom? That lying fuck.'

But he wasn't angry. He was still. He was calm. He didn't know what he was supposed to do now. Who was he supposed to hurt? He watched the reflection of his son's angry eyes. Danny still talking. He heard his son sniff heavily with rage. Expecting something. If there was anyone to hurt, it would be himself. That was how he felt. The worse, the better. Get it done with.

'Those fuckers. All the time you were innocent.'

Innocent. That was a word from inside. Spoken often. Innocent. He didn't know about that. It was always good for a laugh. An ugly laugh. The way they did inside. The way it just burst out of you. When that word was spoken. A laugh changing to something else. Pitting itself against you. Innocent. That word and the look in the eyes of someone new saying it. Then knowing better by the ugly laughter. Never saying it again. Who ever knew for sure? Knew for certain? But it was always good for a laugh.

The houses began to change. The bungalows and older houses with nice yards turned to smaller houses with smaller yards, and then row houses. Doorsteps right on the asphalt curb. No yards. No sidewalks. Children in the street. Playing like they owned the place. Not minding the cars. The cars were meant to watch out. For them. See what happens if you hit me. Go ahead. See where that'll get you. Adults standing in their doorways, watching the cars move by. One or two of them shouting at a child, or raising their hands. To wave. Like they knew him. Like they were waiting to catch sight of him. Danny's car. They must recognize it.

The car pulled up in front of his wife's house. He looked at the door release. Took hold of it with his bent fingers that ached. Broken too many times. He pulled the handle. Springs and steel clicking. Uncomplicated machinery. Easy to open. Easy to break. He could get out of this with a push. The door swung open. Too hard. He hadn't meant that. Swung right open. No one standing there to take his arm. To make certain. It swung back on him. He stopped it with his hand.

He stepped out. The bottoms of his shoes flat to the asphalt. Air above and around him. Space shooting off in all directions. Space fitted round him. Shooting off in all directions.

He lifted his arms in front of him. Moved them without knowing. Saw his hands. But didn't look right at them. What to do with his hands out here?

His son, Danny, slapped him on the shoulder and went ahead.

He followed to the sound of car doors slamming

behind him. People hurrying. Chasing after him. Calling out already.

The door to his wife's house was thrown open. A crowd of people waiting there, shouting, 'Welcome home,' 'Surprise.' He heard more car doors slam. Turned to see vans and cars stopped in the narrow street, blocking traffic. Cameras and microphones. Reporters up close now, shouting questions. Mister Myrden? His name, a question. What do you think of a penal system that . . . ? Mister Myrden? How do you feel about . . . ? Mister Myrden? Who do you think really killed her? Mister Myrden? If you had your time back . . .

Danny took his shoulder and nudged him ahead. Into the house. He knew most of the people who welcomed him. The years still kept them a certain way. They patted him on the back. Touched his arms and hands. Wished him well. His wife hanging onto him. Hugging too hard. Her bony grip strong for such a small woman. She'd come to see him inside. Once a month maybe. Tell him what he had done wrong. Why he was in there. Tell him about her problems. He'd watch her, wondering who she was. What she wanted.

Now, she was hugging him. Squeezing his arm. Laughing back at the crowd. 'Innocent as the lamb,' she said to everyone. 'Knew it all along.'

His granddaughter, Caroline, held up her arms and he

grabbed her and took her off her feet. He knew her only. From a picture on his wall. That was it. All he ever knew of her. Surprised at how light she was. A small body like that. Nothing that small in fourteen years. Kissed her soft cheek. Nothing so small inside. She hugged him hard. Held on like she was the desperate one. Until he was weeping and the others went a little quiet. Helped him through it with bits of conversation.

The door shut behind him. The reporters locked outside.

But he couldn't get his mind off them. With the party still going on, he'd look out the front window. Saw them out there. Even in the dark. They stayed in the cars and vans with the dome lights on. Watching his wife's house.

'Here,' his old best friend, Randy, said above the fiddle music and chatter. 'You can't be left standing tonight.' Randy laughed the way he always did. Like a bunch of barks strung together. Nothing ever bothered him. Top three buttons of his shirt undone. Silver cross on a silver chain. His hair cut short. His thin face with the scrap of a beard. Bright eyes always searching.

He looked to see a beer bottle held toward him. He already had one in each hand. Randy stuck the bottle between his elbow and side.

'There,' Randy shouted and turned to make sure people were watching because they kept watching him all the time. They laughed and raised their drinks. Beer bottles. Rum and cola in glasses. No ice. All the faces with their eyes on him. To see what he was thinking. What he might do next.

It was too much.

Randy nodded at his wife. 'Getting some conjugals tonight.' Laughed easy. Raspy.

He took another swig of beer. Felt a little better. The beer tasted good but not the same. Something out of whack with everyone in the room. Something missing. Something wrong. Everyone too close together. Not keeping to themselves. In a row. On a unit. Lockdown. And those people outside the window. What they all knew about him being innocent. Who believed it? A technicality. That's all. One of the men inside had said. Standing over him. Body pumped hard. Muscles like rock letting nothing past. Hit me to see how hard. Hit me. Harder. Spitting. Hating him. Kicking him. Hit me harder. A technicality, you.

When he woke in the morning, he cleared his throat and shut his eyes again. The taste in his mouth was foul. He'd forgotten the bullying weight of a hangover. What did he regret now? That was the only question. A hangover. What did he regret now? His hands began to hurt. He looked at one. Knuckles covered in dark, dried blood.

Stains and fresh scabs. He made a sound, then checked his other hand. Those knuckles the same. His wife was beside him, facing away. He rose with fright and looked at her. He remembered with dread that his hurt knuckles had something to do with her. He leaned over. Careful not to touch. Her face was fine though. He waited to see that she was sleeping.

The fight had been with a man. It had been about his wife. There was noise in his head. The fear of going back in. The dead-tight clang of doors. He rose from the bed and went to the bathroom to vomit. Soaked in sweat and up from his knees, he looked out the small bathroom window. Leaned closer to see down there. A view of the street. Vans and cars waiting. This was not the place for him. He wanted a smaller room where everything was easy to manage. Less people. Not so many things to put in order. He began shivering. His fingers rattling the windowpane. There was a noise from downstairs. Footsteps coming up. Then Randy, standing in the bathroom doorway. A beer bottle in each hand.

'Breakfast,' Randy said with a grin that opened up his mouth and the hole where he had lost his front teeth. A fight twenty years ago. He had knocked those two teeth out of his old best friend's mouth. It didn't matter now. 'Eat up.'

He took the bottle from Randy. It wasn't cold. His

hand shook a little. But it wasn't from the booze. It was from something else. Something deeper than that. Something frightening.

'It goes like this.' Randy tipped back his bottle, chugging down the beer. All the while watching him. Wondering about him. Wanting him to do the same because he was free now. And that's the way it should be. Free until the bottle was empty.

'Ahhh,' said Randy when he was done. The bottle drained. A big grin. A wink. Be a man.

He took a sip. It fizzed up in his mouth. Piss-warm. He spat it in the toilet.

He remembered his granddaughter, Caroline, and he was brokenhearted with shame. Had she left before the fight? He hoped she had. It must have been later at night. There was a gap in his memory that the booze had washed out. A flood over earth. He had been trying to talk with his granddaughter all night. But others had taken him away from her. Others who wanted thoughts on his feelings. How much did he hate those people? What was he going to do to Grom? Who really killed her then? That woman. What was her name again? Doreen Something? That night. Who did it? Eyes on him. They all had thoughts on it. Easy thoughts for them.

His daughter, Jackie, mother of his granddaughter, had

been worried. She feared him. She did not want his granddaughter too near him because she feared him. That was what had made him angry. He remembered. That was the beginning. His daughter at that distance. Far away from him. Guarding Caroline. Then the talk of the man who had been seeing his wife. Fourteen years. What's it like to be out? What's it like to be free? A whisper to him. More talk of the man who had been seeing his wife. Eyes cast toward the man. What are your plans? You'll get a million bucks now. Maybe two million. Do what you want. Anything. Laughter in the mouth. Wide-open. Spread-eagle. Or even three million. Like what they gave what's-his-name. They owe you. Then more talk about his old friend, Manny Grom. Witness to the murder. Manny Grom was looking for him. Didn't Grom make it all up? Didn't he? Grom. The bastard. He'll get his now. You'll show him. Lying fucker. He'll be put away instead. He'll get his.

Where was his granddaughter? His daughter had taken her away from him. What's it like to be out? To be free? Manny Grom. And there was Alex. Alex Gilbert. Over there in the corner. The man who had been seeing his wife. What's it like to be out? Christ. It must be just great. The bastards. Hatred and celebration. There was Alex sitting in the corner. Sipping his beer. Not knowing what to think. Sipping his beer. Waiting. Watching. Saying nothing. Alex full of fear because he was out now. Not in for life after all. When you saw a man afraid like that what did you do? What was the thing to do? The best thing. The easiest thing. It filled him with rage. That frightened man. His granddaughter gone. Manny Grom. What're your plans? You'll be rich now. They owe you. Took away your life. Fourteen years. They stole it. Fourteen years. The fuckers. Kick the shit out of Grom. What's it like to be let out?

Go. Now. Get him.

'I don't know' was how he answered the cameras and microphones the day he was released. That's all he said. All he gave them. 'I don't know' answered everything. The next morning. In the corner store. A headline in the newspaper: MYRDEN UNCERTAIN OF PLANS FOR FUTURE.

The store owner, Old Mister Jackman, was extra friendly to him.

'Seen your picture,' he said. Nodding toward the papers. A stack of them on a rack. 'In the *Globe and Mail*, too. Front page. A celebrity.' Jackman grinned and winked. 'Must be great to be out.' Jackman's eyes saying more: What a shame.

He nodded and laid a five-dollar bill on the counter. Money for his roll of antacids.

'That's okay,' said Old Mister Jackman. Pushing the

bill back at him. Glancing toward the glass windows where a bunch of cameras and microphones were waiting.

'Thanks.' He pocketed the bill and tore open the antacids. Popped two into his mouth. Chewed them into chalky pulp. Moved it around with his tongue.

'Hard night last night.'

He made a noise of agreement.

'Big party, I bet.'

He made another sound. Turned to look at the doorway that opened. He thought it might be the cameras and microphones pushing their way in. But it was just two boys with eyes on him. Looking at him. Like he was cut or something. Gawking.

'It's buddy from TV,' one said to the other.

'Hey, buddy,' said the other. 'Got a quarter?'

He nodded. Gave the kid a quarter. The kid looked at the quarter. Like it was from outer space.

He went outside.

The cameras and microphones kept asking questions. He didn't answer. Most of the questions were the same. Asked again and again. Over and over. Like everything had been forgotten right away.

'What do you have to say to your family about the life you've chosen to live?'

The question stopped him dead in his tracks.

'You have a granddaughter, don't you?' A woman's voice.

He turned to look for the voice. The others called louder. Mister Myrden? Mister Myrden? Him facing them like that. It excited them. He could not find the voice until he heard the word granddaughter again. Saw the woman with short brown hair and small-framed glasses. He fixed his eyes on her. She was dressed like she knew better. He took a step toward her. The others got out of his way. Went quiet.

'What do you have to say to your granddaughter about the life you've chosen to lead?'

He thought about the question. The life you've chosen to lead. His granddaughter. It made no sense to him. But it made him angry just to hear it. The hurt in his ears. The throb growing.

'Are you concerned that your sons and daughter will continue with your lifestyle? Your granddaughter, too.' The woman looked at a pad of paper in her hand. She was in her twenties. Full of what she thought was true. She knew about everyone. Every thing. Her other hand held a small tape recorder. Aimed his way. 'One of your sons is in prison. One dead. Driving while impaired. His girlfriend, too. Killed in the same crash. Your other two sons have long histories of offenses.'

That's only four. What about his eldest? Mac. On the

mainland. He started to ask. But stopped himself. Why should this woman know? Who said she was allowed to know about him? Mac who owned his own business. Made a life for himself. What about him? The woman knew nothing about Mac. Or she didn't want to mention him for some reason. Only the facts that would help her. The shit. He stared at the woman. A small woman with dry lips. No makeup. She seemed mad at him.

'What are you saying?' he asked. Cameras went off around him. Video cameras came closer. Microphones in his face. The people got worked up.

'Your sons all have criminal records. What do you say to them?'

He stared hard at her. What about Mac? No criminal record. What about Jackie? A good girl.

'And your granddaughter. Her name is Caroline, isn't it? Don't you worry for the way she'll turn out? For the way little Caroline will turn out.'

He stared at the small woman. He thought he might reach out and smack the tape recorder from her small hand. Caroline. That name in the woman's mouth. Spat out. His lungs were stinging. He had to breathe more. Through his nose. He had to open his mouth. Breathe that way, too.

'Don't you fear for your children, Mister Myrden? What can you tell them? What advice?'

The tape recorder. Other microphones. No one saying a word. These people all not saying a word. Their faces watching his face. His face in the camera lens. Looking from one place to the other. His face back at him. He couldn't stand what he saw.

'What do you want to tell them about your life?' The woman kept on going. Trying to dig into him. Trying to pull words out. 'Your mother was killed when she was forty-six. Killed by your father.'

The microphones in his face. Closer. Their feet on the pavement. Waiting for a reaction from him. The cameras going off faster. His face changing. He could feel it. He tried to find the words. Not the ones she wanted. His lips just twisted. His shoulders bunched together. He looked at the other faces watching him. Men and women. Silent and watching him or checking their recorders. Not a single one of them decent. Anything to further the pain. Anything. He shook his head and sniffed. Turned and walked away. The voices and shouts came again with their questions. Trailing after him.

He had made many things for his granddaughter when inside. Glued together bits of wood and put wheels on them. He had made other things with his hands. Thinking his hands were doing good by the thought of her little face. Her look of wonder when he gave them over. The guards kept the things for him. They put them in a locker. Nothing was allowed in his cell. He left it all in there. Take nothing out of there. How could he have believed it was possible? To take something out of there. What had he been thinking? Something from in there for his granddaughter. In her hands. It made him sick to think of it.

Randy was still at his wife's house. He was eating chicken from a bone. He raised his eyebrows. 'Who you gonna kill today? You got a few lovelies to pick from.' Randy grinned. Laughed like a rough cough. A cigarette going in the ashtray while he ate.

He wondered about Randy. The smart kid in school. Always the smart kid. Smart kid in with the tough kids. Trying to hide it.

His wife was still asleep.

'You wanna go somewhere?' Randy asked.

'Yeah.'

'Gun shop? Knife shop?' Randy wiped his face with a paper towel. 'Bazooka shop?' Still chewing. He took longer than usual to make a point. Swallowed. 'Good chicken. Right friendly, too.' He raised his cigarette. Plucked a draw from it. Pinched the filter between his fingernails. The tip orange-hot and pointed.

He went to the shopping mall. Randy drove him. Drove fast. The reporters couldn't keep up. Randy laughed at them. Watched in the rearview. He laughed with his mouth wide open.

'I should've been a stuntman.'

'I thought that's what you were.' He smiled a little. For the first time in years.

'Yes,' cheered Randy. 'There's the man I used ta love. Don't break my heart like that no more. Running off ta live on a sunny desert isle.'

The car bucked to a stop. Someone crossing in front of them. An angry look. Shopping bags hanging from both hands. A job well done.

'I stopped, didn't I?' said Randy.

The angry face still with its eyes on them.

'I didn't kill ya.' Quickly rolling down his window. Calling out: 'Get over it.' Watching the angry face moving off. Faster. Across the parking lot to a line of cars. 'Yeah, you better run. I got a murderer in here.' He tossed his thumb toward the passenger seat. 'Bloodthirsty.' Then to him: 'You're thirsty, aren't ya?'

'Your mouth is something.' He looked through the car window. The entrance to the mall. People with packages. They bought clothes in there. Stereos. Can-openers. Furniture. They went to the mall for everything. And they came out with something. Always had to. Why would you go there if not to bring something home? To fill up space.

'I'll wait here. My head won't take kindly to that.'
Randy tipped his chin toward the mall. 'You go buy yourself something pretty. With frills. And pick up a bottle
of hair dye while you're at it. You know I prefer blondes.'

'Don't wait. I'll walk.'

'Walk! Are you fucking nuts?'

'I'll walk.'

'Yeah, I guess you are fucking nuts.' Randy looked at
his legs. 'You want to use them? It's a wonder they still
work. I heard 'em squeaking last night. Your elbows
too.'

He opened the car door. Got out. Shut it behind him.
Walked toward the wall of doors. People going past.
Flashing by. A few sets of eyes on him. Most knowing
nothing of who he was. Not in person. Different in
person. Others catching an idea. The shock of a story in
him. Going home to tell who they had seen. Right there.
On his way into the shopping mall. He was alone. By
himself. Going shopping. Yeah. Shopping. Imagine!
Wonder what he could possibly be buying.

The colours on the toy boxes made him shut his eyes.
The lights were too bright. The colours went in his head
and smeared. Washed around like in water. He opened
his eyes. Squinted. Looked down the long aisle. People
wandering while their eyes searched the shelves. Some

pushing carts. Tossing things in. Others stood staring. Not really seeing. Not knowing what was in their heads.

He picked up a box. Its plastic front made noise. He wanted to get at what was inside. The box was taped shut. One strip of tape over the flap. Stuck like nothing else. What kind of tape was that? He tried opening the box with his fingernails. The tape was still stronger than he thought. Tape made out of what? The box was red and yellow and white. It made a lot of noise. Too much. He tore it open. Ripped the box in half and looked at the plastic toy in his hands. It made a squeaking and dinging noise. One button. Another button. All of them with letters on them. The box at his feet. He kicked it up the aisle. It hit a woman's boot. She looked at him. Her face just plain. Not angry. Not mad. Just looking at him. Then she turned away and left.

His face was burning. This place was making him furious. He hated this place. He picked up a new box. He was shaking his head at the cash register. He was breathing heavy. People in the lineup looked at him. His eyes stung. This close to tears. He took money from his pocket. Pieces of paper. How much? He handed money to the woman after waiting too long. Much too long. Why? He kept saying in his head. Why? All these people in a line. His heartbeat hating him.

'Thank you,' said the woman. She handed him his

change. She handed him the bag. It rattled worse than the box. He could barely touch it. The longer he gripped it in his fist. He had to stop on the way home and lay it down. Was almost afraid to pick it up again each time.

What did you buy? What's in the bag? Mister Myrden? Who'd you go shopping for? It's a toy. Isn't it? I can see through the plastic. Who's the toy for? Your grand-daughter? For Caroline. He slammed the door on the cameras and microphones. The sound boomed in the floorboards. Then it was his wife's voice. 'Your lawyer called. He said you should get at it.'

'What?' He took off his coat. Hung it up.

'At suing the government.' She was in the hallway by the door. She'd been waiting for him. 'Grom came over, too. Brazen as anything. Tell him to come see me, he said, like nothing was the matter. They all talked to him.' She pointed to the door.

He looked down at the package.

'What's that?' she asked.

'For Caroline.'

His wife grabbed it up. He looked at her hair. The way it wasn't brushed or combed. The way her face had changed in fourteen years. The way he saw her had changed. He didn't even know her. His wife tore the bag open where it was stapled. She stared down into the bag. 'She got one of those already. That's for babies. Caroline's seven.'

He walked past his wife toward the kitchen. A thirst had come over him. He wanted a drink of water.

'Call your lawyer,' she said after him. 'You got any money on you?'

He took what he had out of his pocket. Laid it on the counter. His wife snatched it up. Like it was hers. She counted it.

'Where'd you get this?' It was almost funny. The way she held it up.

'They gave me it,' he said.

'Who?'

'When I left.'

'Got out.' She laughed without hearing an answer. 'That's all? We'll see about that.'

He could see his reflection in the window above the sink. He smoothed his hair down. Wished he had a comb. He turned on the tap. Water poured out. He dipped his head toward it and put his lips to the flow. Tasted it. The same water from the same place. Wherever that was. It tasted identical.

'Use a fucking glass,' his wife said. 'Didn't they teach you no manners in there?'

*

'They made a mistake, didn't they, Poppy?'

He nodded from his chair at the kitchen table. His granddaughter was almost knee to knee with him. Her chair pulled close. Her face was the most beautiful thing he had ever seen in his entire life. Just beautiful. He couldn't stop looking at it. All of it. The little bits. The tiny things it did. The smooth skin. It was just hers. And the way she needed to know. It was important to her. Knowing.

'It was good that they said they made a mistake.'

'Yes.'

'Mommy said it was a good thing.' She got up and pulled her chair even closer. It took her a while to manage it with the thin blanket wrapped around her. The blanket was red with flowers all over it. Mostly yellow flowers. It was a small life she was leading. Small things. Small thoughts that were pure as anything.

He looked to the side where his daughter, Jackie, was making supper. She stood at the counter. She had made him promise not to drink. Then he could come over. See Caroline. It was right for her to tell him what to do now. He didn't mind because he knew that she was right. What did she know about it? How much? The mess he was in. She was peeling carrots. With a peeler in her hands. Then a knife. Cutting pieces out of them. Not coin-shaped but strips. That's how she made soup. The difference. Her long brown hair was in a ponytail and her ears were pierced a bunch of times. The kitchen was small. Almost cold. Hard to heat. Old row houses. No insulation. He remembered the same about his wife's house. Hearing that on visits. His wife complaining about the cold. It's warm in here though, she'd said. Nice and warm. He remembered her saying that for a long while. It stuck in his head.

Jackie's house was small and not the place for her. His daughter was different. She had a different mind. She was more like his mother. More like his eldest, Mac. Then he remembered it wasn't Jackie's house. His wife had told him. It was Willis's house. They lived together now. It was something he did not want to believe.

'I . . .' He had begun to tell his granddaughter that he had made things inside for her. Always. A memory was just that. Exact. Of her. Thinking while he made things. She kept him going. He knew he'd never see her in there. Jackie wouldn't bring her to that place. And he didn't want her there. It would kill him to watch her through glass. Her watching him behind glass. Wondering what that meant.

'What?' Caroline asked.

'I used to think of you all the time.' His fingers touched her fingers. Little fingers. Smooth. Perfect. The way they worked. 'I had your picture from school up on my wall.'

'That's nice.' She stood and hugged him. Kept holding on. Her eyes shut. A smile on her lips.

He didn't deserve any of it. He noticed his daughter had turned because of his voice. Her hands stopped cutting carrots against the counter. She was staring at him. What was she making? Soup. Homemade. What was he doing there? He stood and took a deep breath.

'Gotta go,' he said.

'No,' said his granddaughter. Her chair fell back because she tried to block his way. Jackie flinched at the bang. 'I won't let you.' His granddaughter grabbed hold of him. Dropped the blanket wrapped around herself. She stood on his feet and hugged him hard. Her feet on his boots. The boots they had given him when he left. Brand new. They knew the right size. Everything about him. Shirt size. Pant size. Family history. Medical history. 'You're not allowed to leave. You have to stay here forever.'

There had been no invitation to supper. His daughter, Jackie, never asked him to stay. She never did. Because of what might happen. The food smelled good. A house full of real home smell. Like no other smell. He had to leave. To walk. The cameras and microphones were outside. His daughter took Caroline and held her in her arms. Took her away from the door.

Backed down the hallway. Not to be near the door when he opened it.

'What did you tell her, Mister Myrden? What did you want in there? Did you warn her?'

A nice ending to the story. That's what they wanted. They wanted it wrapped up. They wanted it done with. It turned out well. Feel good. It ended in tragedy. Feel bad. But a lesson learned. We have all the information. We know everything. We have shown you. The little girl has been warned. Do not go down that path. We have informed you.

He used to watch TV inside. A small screen in his cell. Five-inch was all they were allowed. It was a waste of time. Other people's lives. Nothing ever real. Only made for TV. The people knew they were on there. Nothing natural about it. Reality. Television. Acting. People dressing for TV. In real life. Talking for TV. In real life. Acting for TV.

He hurried away. He knew the streets and yards and lost the reporters. They were impossible. What they asked. To fit it into what they wanted. Nothing he could ever understand. Only what they thought he should understand. Answers to their questions based on their lives. What did they know about asking questions?

Then there was Grom's house. He'd been thinking about the location. It was close. He knew that. And it

was there now. Off to the left. Grom's backyard. Behind
a fence. Wally Fulton's yard. Through there. He'd spent
his life knowing everyone. Every square foot. A child
facing an adult. Who to fear. Who was kind. Who would
beat you. Take you inside. Scare you. Who would crack
open a beer for you. The daughters of this one. The sons
of that one. They were no part of anything. The ones to
punish. Or the ones to get in with. The neighbourhood
was just the same. A colour changed here and there. One
kid looking grown and like his father. Another grown
and looking like her mother. A baby in her arm. On her
hip. He saw the old faces in the new faces. Growing to
be the same. Faces in the windows. On the doorsteps.
Always watching the street. Who was coming. What
would happen next.

A dog was barking in the yard.

He didn't know the dog. It was full-grown but it wasn't
big. Not like its bark. The dog didn't bother him when
he ducked through where three rotten boards left a hole.
The fence leaning. Soon to fall over on its own. The dog
was on a chain. A bunch of ribs sticking out. The mutt
just wanted to get loose. All its life.

He walked right up to it. The barking stopped. The
mutt stretched its neck forward. Eyes never leaving his.
Nervous. A snout sniffed at his leg. There was no bark
then. It backed away. Hunkered down to the ground.

Low. Its soft ears went back. Sad eyes looking up. Its head pressed tight to the ground. Body expecting something. The mutt rolled over to show him its pink belly.

He bent down and rubbed it. The dog jammed shut its eyes when he reached out. Flinched. Not much fur on its body. No meat either. Wasted. The clip came off easy. All that was keeping the dog there. He looked at it. A steady shiver. Its eyes still shut. He rubbed some more. Stroked the clumps of fur. The big eyes opened and it sat up quick. Like someone had called its name. Had been made familiar just like that. Known him all its life. The mutt stood up. Its front paws on his knee. Licked his face. He kept rubbing. Tried not to laugh. It licked his face some more and he tried turning away. There was a window by the back door. Grom's old mother stood there. Watching out. She made a shout and turned away from the window. Gone.

The back door was unlocked. His hand on the knob. People never knew. The dog followed him in.

He heard Grom's mother talking fast. He stepped through the kitchen and into the hallway. Grom's mother came out of the living room. Wheezing. She hated him was how she looked. She'd heard of him. That was all it took.

Light footsteps on the stairs.

He saw a boy leaning over the rail. The boy watched him. The boy didn't seem to care. He was just there to see.

'What you want?' Grom's voice called out. A boom from a hollow.

The boy stared. Nothing to worry about yet. An everyday thing.

'Dun't ye lay a finger on him.' Grom's mother stayed close when he stepped further into the hallway. Right by his side. Wagging her finger. Breathing raspy. She couldn't get much closer. She was grey-haired with a shriveled face. She moved when he moved. Her body almost touching his. Staring up at him. Blinking. Sucking her lips into her mouth. Wagging her finger. Then she saw the dog follow him in.

'No dog,' she said. Bending and hitting the dog. Grunting. Whacking it. Like it wasn't meant to be at all. 'No dog, no dog . . .'

The dog yelped and skittered back to the door. 'No dog 'n here. Filth.'

Footsteps came down the stairs. He heard them as he went into the living room.

Grom was on the couch. Fat as ever. Fourteen years. The man who had testified. Against him. Put him away. Now his testimony with holes in it. All of a sudden. When they took a good look at it again. When they took a good hard look. When they had a little extra time. His new lawyer said as much. After reviewing the testimony. After taking his case. His old lawyer hadn't cared enough to see.

A young woman called out from upstairs. In warning. A boy's name. Her voice was near screaming like something bad was happening. Shrill was the word. He turned to see the boy not far behind him.

'That's Teddy,' Grom said. Breathing hard. Hard to talk because he was so fat. 'My grandson.'

'He's yer son is who he is,' the mother said to Grom. 'Christ!' She was wheezing harder, back from slamming the door. The dog whining behind a wall. It wouldn't go away. It stayed there. Wanting to be let in.

He sighed and looked at Grom. Grom had three chins and his eyes were puffy. His head was shaved to a crewcut. Brown bags under his eyes. Sick skin. How did he stay alive?

'They told me to make one call,' he said.

'Da police,' said Grom's mother. Nodding. 'I'm calling dem . . . like dey said to.' She backed away. But her eyes stayed on him.

He watched her go to the phone in the corner. Pick it up. Press buttons. She'd done it before. Barely looked at the numbers. There was a trick to it. Her fingers knowing where they should go.

'They'll come for you,' he said to Grom. 'You're a liar.'

'Mom,' Grom called. 'No.' He raised a hand like it was heavy.

Grom's mother hung up right away. Hard. The telephone dinging.

'Fuck off.' It was the boy. 'I know who you are. You fuck right off, now.' He was ten. Maybe eleven. He'd been told things. Whatever suited the occasion.

Grom laughed a little.

He stared at Grom's face. 'Who did it?'

'What? Killed her?' Grom shrugged. 'Wasn't it you?' His stomach jiggled under his stained shirt. 'You were out of your mind. Loaded.'

It was a blank to him. A blank that dropped him deeper when he thought of Doreen Stagg's name. Nowhere for his feet to land. Her face when she was alive. Who had been there? He didn't even know. He couldn't say one way or the other. He knew who he'd started with. Who he'd been drinking with. Grom. Willis. Muss. Squid.

Grom shrugged again. The thing that was wrong with his shoulder. Like a shrug but slower.

'Willis weren't there,' said Grom's mother.

'DNA,' said Grom. 'Ain't that something. DNA's the rat's ass.' He struggled to stand. He tried once. Then he tried again. Heaving and groaning and grabbing at the coffee table. One hand pushing at the back of the couch. The other reaching. His fingers slipping. The boy went and pulled him up. That's all he needed. A little tug.

On his feet. 'Twenty years ago, you'd never know.' Grom came near him. 'DNA.' Stood near him. He smelled of grease. Fish and chips. Ketchup. Vinegar. This close was dangerous. He wished he had something in his hand. Something sharp. Better yet. Something blunt.

The boy stood by Grom's side. The boy said: 'Fuck off or I'll tear the head right off ya.'

He felt something dig into his back and turned around. It was Grom's mother with a crowbar. She poked him hard with the flattened end. Then she raised it. Like a baseball bat held back. Wheezing.

'Get out,' she said. There was white scum on her lips from sucking them. 'Out.' She screeched louder. Barely moving her lips. Nothing to it. Making that sound. 'Get out, or I'll . . . smash yer skull open.'

He could take that crowbar from her. Easy. One grab. His arm like a spring. He had it all bottled up. Let it loose. Let it go. Fourteen years. His wife. Her house. His sons. Doreen Stagg. Snatch hold of the crowbar. Heavy steel swinging through air. Until impact. And again. And again . . . No one left standing then. Not a soul.

The young woman upstairs screamed the boy's name.

The boy ignored her. The boy spit: 'You fucking hear me, prick?'

'Get out.' Grom's mom screeching. Ready to swing.

Grom's dog followed him from the yard. The dog wouldn't get off his heels. He didn't mind. It trotted with him like it knew him forever. Walking. Looking ahead. Looking up at him. Walking.

He thought of Willis. Grom's brother. Willis wasn't there. Grom's mother: Willis weren't there. Yes he was. And he wasn't married to his daughter then. Not married to Jackie like he was now. Was Willis there or not?

He stopped walking. He felt like he was flying. That fast. The glide. He looked around to see where he was. One place to another without knowing. There were cars parked on the street. New models. Some of them not much different. Hubcap-shaped TV dishes on the sides of houses. He'd heard about them. A worn-out place like this. Everything broken. Almost dead. His heart sped a bit. The people near dead. He was scaring himself with the thought. They all looked sick. They were grey. Dead on their feet. He began sweating at the idea. Poverty with five hundred channels. The dog stopped to look up at him. It whined and sneezed. Pawed at its nose. Sneezed again. Ribs sticking out. Fur not so good. How sick was it? Left to itself on a chain.

'What?' he asked the dog. Trying to get back to himself. Trying to get himself back in his body. He felt he did not belong in there. Something at the centre tugging to get out of him. To get free. He had to breathe. Tingling. His heartbeat. His tight throat. He bent down and stared at the dog's face. The short brown and white hair on its muzzle. 'Who're you?' he asked. Rubbing one floppy ear. He almost laughed at the softness. The warmth. This dog. Who was this fucking dog? Talking to it made him feel better. 'You're not right,' he said to the dog. 'What the hell are you?'

He picked the dog up in his arms. It licked his face. That was something. That feeling.

Chapter Two

'It might take a while but there's going to be a full pardon. It's only a question of what legal course you decide to pursue. There'll be a settlement.'

He watched the lawyer. The words were something to listen to. The way the lawyer had learned. Like the thinkers in the pen. Always with books. Always the ones to be around. The ones with the least trouble in them. Not like the strong arms or the cowards.

'Do you want it fast, less money, or slow and more money?'

He wanted money for his daughter, Jackie. For his granddaughter, Caroline. Buy them out of Willis's house. Put them somewhere away from the leech. The bastard. Willis. Fast. He wanted it fast.

'You've got people to look after.'

He nodded.

'Your wife needs taking care of.'

'My granddaughter.'

'Yes, and your granddaughter. That's who needs it, right? We should look after her. Set up a trust. You indicated something along these lines some time ago. What about her father?'

'I don't know.' Thinking about Willis, his knuckles felt itchy. He looked at them. Picked away a scab. Then folded his arms across his chest.

'He's a liability. A problem, right?'

He said nothing. Admitted nothing.

'I'm from that neighbourhood too, remember. Jackie's husband is abusive. I know that. Willis Grom. All the Groms. I've seen them down in court enough times. We'll work to get Willis clear of her. I can apply for a restraining order. I'll need Jackie's consent.'

None of his business. That's none of your business. He wanted to say. But not to this man. Not to the lawyer. The thinker.

'You don't want to give the money to Willis Grom. You and I both know what'll happen to it. If anything, you set up a trust fund in your daughter's name.'

'He'll get it from her.'

The lawyer watched him. The lawyer said nothing. Held a pencil in his hands. Tried to hold it even. Level. In front of his tie. 'You can keep it away from him. You just look after her when you get the money.'

'He gets it too.'

'If they're still together. If he retains a lawyer. There'll have to be a settlement.' The lawyer slapped down the pencil. It bounced on the desk. He shook his head. He snorted in disgust. Then he stood. He put his hands on his hips and looked out the big window that showed him the city. Downtown. Buildings with nothing but windows. People sitting behind them or moving with papers in their hands. Hundreds of people. 'Jackie,' he whispered. His tie was crooked. His suit was a good fit.

'You two grew up together.'

The lawyer looked at him. 'Almost together. I was right on the cusp, the edge. You know what those streets are like. The dividing line. Good neighbourhood. Bad neighbourhood. One street to the next. I remember she was a nice girl.'

He watched the lawyer's face. The telephone buzzed on the desk. They both looked at it.

'What to do about Willis?' the lawyer asked.

He stood and rubbed his hands together. They were cold. His circulation was bad. Something to do with his heart. It was in hard shape. He wouldn't tell a soul. He'd already had two heart attacks in prison. Taken to the hospital. Two guards with him on the cardiac unit. One at the door. One by his bed. But no one knew. Not even his wife. No one outside knew anything about you in there. Unless you wanted. Unless you told them. The heart attacks were nothing. His body shutting down on one side like a switch had been flicked. The leg and arm going on the right side. Then his right eye. Blind. Then he was okay after a while. They did some tests. Wires inside him with tiny cameras. Right into his heart. Said there was nothing to do about it. What would they do anyway? Make him eat food that tasted like paper. The doctors kept talking. One came. Then another. Asking the same questions. He never listened to them when they explained. Only so long. How many ways to say that?

'You cold?'

He shook his head, wiped his cold nose with the side of his thumb.

'You're a little pale.'

He cleared his throat.

'We'll take care of it,' said the lawyer. 'I won't give up on this.'

'I don't have any money.'

'Don't worry. You won't owe me anything until the government settles.'

'No, I don't have any money.'

'For yourself?'

He nodded.

The lawyer reached into his pocket. He took out a fold of twenties. 'How much do you need?' He smiled and it was okay. Not a bad face. Not a mean intention that he could see. 'I'll put it on your tab.'

The cameras and microphones were gone. They had been interested in him. Like they needed to be interested in what he did and thought. It was supposed to be that way. Someone ordered them. Be interested. But they weren't. Not really. He'd think of them now. Their faces. He got to know the faces. They had lives, he supposed. Fast ones. Always keeping busy. Always being in the know. Cellphones going off. They'd turn away from whatever. To answer the latest thing. In their ear. The news. They headed right for it. Looking important in their own heads. Racing for the red light. His father used to say that. When cars went fast. Roared by. Racing for the red light. The cameras and microphones didn't mean they cared. They were just there to fill paper up with words. TVs with pictures. Maybe it was only their job. But it was more than that. They wanted something from him. To take away. To be the first to have it. It made him want to rub his palms together. See what would fall from them. The grime in his lifelines.

They were gone now.

No one outside his door except visitors. People he hardly knew before. People from the street and one or two streets over. People from even farther away. He'd grown up in the neighbourhood. His house lived in by someone else now. Over on Blatch Avenue. He'd lost all that. His wife didn't want any part of it. Sold the house. It was okay with him. He wasn't coming back. He still didn't know who owned his wife's house. Was it hers? Another man's? He didn't care. Rumours. None of it mattered. Stories going around. All sorts. It wasn't important. The thought would come and he'd shut it off. A thought would come that he didn't like. Boom. He'd shut it off. A thought would come that he liked too much. Boom. He'd shut it off.

People came to see him. Sat in the kitchen. They brought beer or rum. They'd ask him about nothing, really. Then they'd ask him what he was going to do with all his money. Buy a big house. I bet. A big car. They'd smile at the thought of it. A chauffeur and limousine. An airplane even. Always that smile. What a stroke of luck. You'll be on Easy Street.

He watched them sitting there. Randy called them the People Making the Pilgrimage to the Holy Shrine of Future Wealth. It made sense to him. Randy's father had been an artist. He remembered Randy's father from when he was a boy. Randy's father sat in a room in the same white T-shirt and black pants worn to a shine. He watched out the window. He painted what he saw. That's what it was like. Randy's father watching out the window. Then putting the paintbrush to the paper. Painted what he saw. Then watched out the window. But what he painted was never what was outside the window. It was all cut up. Shifted. Weird and twisted. Like there was something the matter with his eyes. Like they were cut to pieces and saw that way. Randy's father died when Randy was a teenager. Hit by a taxi. Drunk at night. Singing in the streets. From a man who never said a word. Not a word to anyone. Until he hit the bottle. Belting out some song about losing. Singing the way Randy sang in the streets now. Until Randy's father was struck. One foot off the curb. The song punched out of him.

His wife was on the phone in the living room. Talking about him. His plans. Everyone wanted to know. They'd get around to the money. His wife laughed. She changed when she talked about the money. She touched her hair. She touched her lips. She became delicate. Respected by herself.

'Isn't that the case?' an old man sitting at the table said. 'Isn't that always the case? They never get anything right. The friggin' government. But you're okay now. Ain't ya?' The old man reached ahead and slapped his leg. 'You're the finest kind now.'

The dreams locked him back in there. All a mistake. Like someone was really dead, but really wasn't. Everything a mistake. In. A mistake. Out. A mistake.

Incarceration. People telling him it was a mistake. Putting him in. Letting him out. He could weep when he woke up. He was on the edge of it. He had no peace. His body wouldn't let him believe anything. Worked against him.

Any moment now. They'll come for him.

He looked toward the kitchen entranceway. Who would step through the opening? The house. He looked at the kitchen window. The old man was still talking. He took a swallow of beer. The window. Outside there was another house close. Only enough space to squeeze through turned sideways. The house was yellow.

The dog shifted under the table. That dog from Grom's would never leave his side. Followed him to the bathroom. Watched up at him. Slept by his bed. Stayed close. Turned to butter when you scratched its ears.

Willis.

He was afraid of Willis.

Footsteps came into the kitchen. Randy. Winking at him and the old man.

'Who's ready for action?' Deep draw on his cigarette. The laugh with the front teeth missing.

He finished his beer. Laid the bottle down on the table.

'Who's this pilgrim?' Randy asked. 'I don't know you.'

The old man took a little time turning. His back or neck was busted up. He tried to see the face. Curious.

'Randy Murphy,' said the old man with a white denture smile. Lips pulled right back. Tight. Plump cheeks.

'Who're you?' Randy laughed.

'I'm Paddy French.'

'Christ, I never set eyes on you before. Are you sure you're Paddy French?'

'From Casey Street.'

'Now you're having a beer,' Randy said. 'Having a good time. If you was having any better a time you'd be dancing, I bet.'

'Yes.' Another thin-lipped smile. A wheezy chuckle. 'Having a beer and a good time with himself.'

He did not want to be a nuisance. But the only thing that mattered was his daughter, Jackie, and his granddaughter, Caroline. The beer made it worse. Three or four bottles. Five or six. He needed something then. Impossible to know what it was. Impossible to stop him. Her house came nearer. She kept a lovely house despite the little she had. He imagined she would have a better house. If his money came through. One she could do lots with. A good house with nice smells in it. Clean and new. Just built. Fresh lumber. Fresh paint. No rot in the floor. No rot around the windows. No mice on the kitchen counter. No rats chewing inside the walls.

'I'm not going in,' said Randy.

'Who asked you?'

'That was my exact point.' He laughed like he did after everything he said. The car pulled over. In front of Jackie's house.

He got out and heard the shouting right away. The booming echo of a body hitting wood. The houses on the streets all connected. You could feel that sort of thing if you were five houses down. The rumble. Day or night. He knocked on the door. No one answered. Shouting inside. A man. A woman. A little girl crying. Little voice screaming. Stop.

The door flung open. A hole that he stepped through. A hole that he stepped into. His movements rushed right through him. Inside. Back in the kitchen. Before he knew it. The house like his wife's. Same layout. Built the same. Neater. Done up nice. A man with a woman by the hair. A little girl screaming. Slapping at the man. Little hands. Balled into little fists. He was in the kitchen. Right away. All eyes on him. The noise he was making. The roar. Willis let go of his daughter's hair. She fell to her knees. Breath shocked out of her. One rush. Not even footsteps. One rush forward. Got Willis by the throat. One hand. Dead tight grip on the throat. Not a speck of air getting in. His daughter, Jackie, crying by the table. Willis up off his feet. His granddaughter, Caroline, watching him. His hand on the throat. The feet up off the ground.

'Daddy,' said his granddaughter. 'Daddy.' She was talking about Willis.

'Leave him,' said his daughter. Now up on her feet. Back on her feet. Up off the floor. Standing there. Tears shut down. Reasonable. A mother. A wife. Do what was expected. 'Stop it, Dad.' Who was the enemy now.

'Daddy,' screamed Caroline. 'Daaaaddyyy . . .'

His hand tight on the throat. The feet up off the floor. What was best for everyone. Willis's arms losing their strength. Letting go. Dangling. Useless.

Jackie's face. The bruise. The blood on her lip. Her licking it away. 'Stop it.' On the verge of something else. Mad at him.

He tightened the grip. Fingers. Knuckles. Bones. How horrible and good was it.

'Daaaaaaaaddyyy!' Caroline shrieking.

The feet kicking around up off the floor. Banging the wall. Slow. Slower. Then harder.

'Stop it, Dad,' Jackie shouted. 'You're hurting him.'

He was shaking and his heart wouldn't stop. Noise pounding in his head. Not the noise and screaming in the house before. His head. He couldn't catch his breath. His lungs burning. His heart would not settle. He was sitting in Randy's car. Out in front of the house. Breathing to steady himself. Waiting for his leg to die.

His arm. His eye. It never. It was just the pounding. The pain.

Randy watched through the windshield. His hands on his lap. He didn't know what to do. The car was still running. Randy went to say something. But it never came out.

He squeezed his fists together. Breathed through his nostrils. His heart would not quiet down.

'Where you want to go?' Randy asked. Like he was disappointed. A date gone bad. His fingers were on the keys. He was going to turn the car off. Or maybe he forgot it was already running. His eyes were on the windshield. Then Randy's eyes were on his chest.

He tried to get some spit together in his mouth. Swallow. His heart still punching. Popping in his eardrums. The back of his head. His neck. Sweat in his eyebrows. He swiped it away.

Randy sat there. Waited. Looked through the windshield again. His eyes checking around. Seeing out but not seeing what was there. Like his old man. Randy grabbed for the door handle. Went to rush out.

He grabbed Randy's arm. 'Don't,' he said. His face was stinging. There were marks on his cheek. The left one. His daughter's fingernails. Jackie's fingernails. What had he made her do. Stop it, she'd screamed. Leave him

alone. His daughter and his granddaughter. Caroline. Let
go of him. Fingernails in his face. It wasn't her fault.

'Let's go,' he said.

Randy sat back in his seat. He pulled down the transmission stick. He just drove ahead. He didn't ask where
to. The car went forward. It stopped. It went around a
corner. Cars and houses moving past outside the window.
None of it with any meaning.

Randy said nothing.

He said nothing.

'Should I be driving faster?' Randy asked.

'No.' The heart in his chest began to quiet.

'He's still breathing then.'

He nodded.

They drove around for a while. Both of them watching
straight ahead. Randy lit a cigarette and plucked a draw
from it. He plucked more draws from it. Thinking hard.
Then he put it out. Crushed it out.

'That's too bad,' Randy said. But who knew what it
meant.

'Jackie called,' said his wife when he came in the door.
Angry. Fed up with him. Living in her house. Beating people
up. Causing grief. Ruining things for everyone. 'She doesn't
want you at her house anymore. What'd you do to Willis?'

He went to the fridge and poured a glass of milk. His

wife was on the kitchen phone. She was sitting at the table smoking a cigarette. Blue haze of smoke hanging in the air. She pressed the receiver against her chest. Sound blocked. A few private words between them. With someone on the other end. Waiting.

The glass of milk was cold. He could feel it going all the way down. Inch by inch. Brightening his insides. He looked under the table for the dog. It wasn't there. Gone. Who cared.

'Caroline was scared to death.'

He turned before he knew it. And the glass exploded over the table. His wife ducked away. Her mouth shut now. One look at her. You're not hurt. His father's voice in his head. His father's eyes not even checking. A quiet voice then. Believe me. You're not hurt.

Outside. The air was cold on his face. He walked fast. He made the turn. He knew the street. It was the same as he remembered. Exactly. Like anything. Like a long walk down a corridor. Looking straight ahead. But knowing everything to all sides. Houses. Cells. Windows. People inside. Watching out. Time dead in their eyes. He knew the right direction. Looking straight ahead. The exact way to go.

What they'd found on him wasn't hers after all. DNA. The hairs. They belonged to another woman. Not from the body. He was going back there. Going for Willis. That's where he would go. Where he needed to go. Self-defense was how it should be. With Willis. He knew about Willis now.

But it didn't happen. He just passed by Willis's house. His ears listening. His eyes on the ground. There was no sound. By the window. It was quiet. He crossed the street. Stood at the end of the road. Hands in the pockets of his coat. He watched Willis's house. Jackie and Caroline in there. In that man's house. Living together. Everything silent. Who knew what to say now. Everything quiet. Everyone alone with themselves. Dulled. No one hurt. He wanted to go in there. Willis's house. A blue house between two yellow ones. All in a row. He was breathing through his nostrils. Hard enough to hear. He watched the door. The window with nice curtains. The doorknob. Thinking of them in there. Not saying a word. Afraid or ashamed. Just the silence. The slow healing toward more pain.

He made himself walk off.

Down the hill toward downtown. The graveyard. Down the hill where the graves sloped toward the city. Then a few big buildings sticking up. They'd built around the graves. He used to visit there. He hated visiting it. Felt he needed to. Something he was supposed to do. Out of respect. His father. What was there to see in the stone? People stood at graves in the cold. Eyes staring. Heads filled up. Hands in pockets. A woman pressed a tissue to her pink nose. A hat on her head that matched her long red coat. Black fur collar. Her breath coming out of her in the cold. In there with the baby graves. All of them behind a fence with a gate. Kept separate from the bigger graves. All grown up. What sort of suffering drew people there? Made them keep coming back. What was the fence for? To keep the tiny to themselves? That special misery locked in. He passed her. Passed the bunch of trees. His father lying there in the ground. Right beside his mother. Put her there. Then right beside her. Sleeping in separate beds. But together. Always together. Wed that way. Husband and wife. Born. Died. Safe in the arms of Jesus. Two separate tombstones. He read the etched letters on his father's stone. Read them again. But could not look at his mother's. Could not read the letters. His eyes went there but he would not read. His father's stone. He'd kick it over.

Footsteps came up behind him on the asphalt path. He did not know how long he had been standing there. With what in his head. The footsteps were light. Then they stopped. A smell of perfume. An old woman. He turned to see. Not an old woman at all. But Ruth. Yes, it was. Ruth. Looking at him.

'Ruth,' he said. The woman in the red coat at the baby graves. He thought he recognized something before. Took in the details because of that. Not knowing it was Ruth. Knowing something though. His head alone. Not really himself in here.

She said his name.

He swallowed and she looked back at the baby graves.

Christ, he thought. Jesus Christ, he thought. How horrible for her. What was in that place? Tiny and so big. His skin prickled. If he had any words they would bust open a wall. A well. Tears inside him. Pouring down. But not out. Running down behind his face. Like they would often do. They just wouldn't stop. How long ago? Whose baby?

'I read about you,' she said. 'They made a mistake, hey? Small one.'

He smiled at that because she meant for him to. It was natural to be around her. Just like that. She always treated him that way.

How many years? Twenty. Or more. Her face the same. A little older but the same. She would be forty-one that month. He remembered. November. The eleventh. Six years younger than him. Good-looking. He still loved her face. He could not help it. She had one of those faces. One of the first ones he had ever loved. He could not stop loving it. Ever.

'How are you?' she asked. The breath coming out of her in mist.

'Okay.'

That smile. Little. Tiny. Like that grave. She was afraid of things now. Her eyes told him. Something had done this to her.

He looked around the graveyard. The cool air on his face. Cool on the scratch marks. Almost numbing. The ground hard. Hadn't snowed yet. Not for the winter. Not once. It could though at any moment. Smelled like it. Felt like it.

'You're okay,' she said, checking the scratch marks. Not trying to hide it.

'Yeah.'

And her eyes went to the graves. His parents. And her eyes changed and her smile changed. She was turned by it. Her lips almost souring. Slowly. She knew more about what it meant now. Death had had its way with her. Still did.

He rubbed his hands together without knowing it. Only because she looked there.

'It's cold,' she said.

'Too cold.'

'How tragic, hey?' But she wasn't looking at the graves now. The two big ones he had come for. The small one she had come for. Maybe others too. She looked at his eyes. Right into him. How tragic. It was him she saw. And she knew. She had always known. A bad life. But maybe something more than a bad life. She was that type of woman. Saw things better than they were. But how she saw now was probably not the same. After so many years of seeing.

Ruth came from money. That's what his mother used to say. His mother used to say that. Before she was killed. His mother dead there on the floor. Stopped. His father looking at him. Eyes nothing like eyes.

Ruth's from money. He wanted his mother to know Ruth. His mother would like Ruth. And she did. But it wasn't because of Ruth being from money. He took Ruth to see his mother. They sat down at the kitchen table and talked. His mother in her housedress. Smoking cigarettes. Ruth in a summer dress. A young woman. Listening. They talked for an hour or more. He left them there. He liked the idea of them talking. They fit together. His mother having things to say. Words she couldn't say to anyone on the street.

Ruth was from money. Like a place. A town. A big city. Wheels spinning always. Lights on. Glass. Mirrors. Movement at night. Taxis through the clear darkness. People out strolling. Store windows reflecting. And she was still from money. He could see it in her clothes and the way she talked. The way her lips moved. He had met Ruth's father once. Saw him by accident in a store with Ruth. One look. Ruth's father knew about him. Like Ruth. Only Ruth's father knew different things. Because he was a man. A bad life. Good riddance. He saw the trouble. Ruth saw what she saw because she was a woman. A bad life. How unfair.

'You like sugar?'

He shook his head. He shouldn't have come here. The house was strange to him. He couldn't tell if there was a man. If a man lived in the house too. If that man might come home. Any moment now.

'Milk?'

He nodded. He had dreamt of her for years. Inside. He dreamt of her. He still did. Twenty years later. All those years. What did that tell him?

She sat down across from him. They were in a booth made out of wood in a kitchen made out of wood. It was warm. Well insulated. Comfortable. Drawings of houses were hung on the walls. Drawings of oceans. Drawings of fields. Dried things were hung from the ceiling. Grass or fruit strung together. The place smelled nice. Wood and spices. Jackie would like it. She would stand and take her time looking at things. Stand still and look at the details. Plenty of space to play outside. Little Caroline. Grass that would be soft. Barefoot in the summer. No worry of broken glass. Trees. Just outside the city. Horses up the road. They had passed a stable on the way in the car. Horses out front. Eating or watching them pass. The biggest animal you could keep.

There were things on the wooden table. A bunch of bottles on a tray. For shaking stuff on food. The spice of life. He remembered that from somewhere. The table was put together properly. Someone had taken the time. He had learned about wood inside. About building things. He slowly ran his palm over the top. Good smooth work.

'Are you hungry?' She had on a pretty white blouse. Her hair in a ponytail. Older but still with a ponytail. He liked that. It reminded him of her.

'No.' He sipped his coffee.

'How's your family?'

'Fine.'

'You've got a granddaughter.'

He looked at her eyes. How did she know it? From friends? From the news?

'You think I'm too old now?'

She laughed a little. Different from the graveyard. Almost shy. 'No. Why would I think that?'

'Who knows?' He shouldn't have come. He felt wrong in this place. This house made up of pretend things. A nicer life than what it was. Outside the city.

'What's her name?'

'Caroline.'

Ruth smiled. More and more. 'That's so great.' She reached out. Touched his hand. 'You're cold. I can turn up the heat.' She made to stand.

'No. It's just me.'

'You sure?'

He didn't answer. He was sure.

'I was going to ask what you've been up to.'

'Yeah.' He laughed. Wiped at his bottom lip.

'That's funny?'

'What I've been up to. The usual.' He looked out the window at the end of the booth. The windows were narrow and high. There was a stem you turned to open them. Windows like that were expensive. Big windows. He always liked them. But he had small windows. His old bedroom window. He could barely climb through it as a boy. Barely get out in time.

'You like playing pool. I remember. We used to play.'

'That's right.' He liked the thought of that. The way they had met. In a pool hall downtown. He had been surprised by how she looked. Couldn't keep his eyes off her while he drank his beer. No tight jeans and tight tops like the other girls. Her in a skirt. A loose blouse. There by herself. Happy to be alone, it seemed. Just playing against herself. Not very good at it.

'I've got a table downstairs. In the basement.'

He sipped his coffee. Her having a table here didn't sit right with him. A table in a house. There was something wrong about it. Not like in a bar where anyone could use it. The people who used hers. No one would know how to play. It would be for a joke. Look at me playing pool.

'Let's have a game.'

He sighed. The weight came off his chest. He swallowed more coffee. It was good. But there was a taste in it he didn't know. He drained what was left.

'Want another?'

'No.' He gave her a smile. 'It's fine.' The smile he remembered giving her. It was hers. She saw that.

'Let's shoot some pool then. I've been practicing.'

Playing pool with a woman was not about the game. It was about watching her. Motion. Her body. Bending. Straightening. Her jeans. Her skirt. Her pants. Her blouse. Open at the top. Buttons. Tight across the breasts. Maybe there was music. That changed her body too. Music changed a woman's body. Shooting like she didn't know how to. Having to help her. Teach her. Letting herself be taught. That was what he liked. Touching. Smelling her. Pressing against her. Carefully. He had to keep his hands off her. Her hair. The colour of it. The warmth coming off it. Her skin. Her face. Her eyelashes. Eyelids blinking.

The most delicate things in the world. Trying to watch her face without her knowing. It was a marvel. She was happy when the ball went down. It meant something to sink a ball. Happy like nothing else. Looking at him with a smile. See? He had to stop from just taking her. Right there. But that would get him nowhere. Pissed off when she missed the shot. Banging the bottom of her cue on the floor. Damn. Everything there. This woman. Ruth. The game brought her to life.

It was suppertime when they stopped playing. They had been drinking beer for a while. He liked that she liked beer. Not the fruity drinks. Bright colours. Sugar. Bottled for kids. Nothing to them. She had different beers to try. Red ones. Black ones. Cream ones. She put them in his hand and he tried them. Interested in the tastes. A day that began to feel right.

Then Ruth took him on a tour of the house. She was unsteady a few steps. Being too happy. Not happy at all. Just a bit. Hiding something else. A life of it. Things he did not know yet. This house. Hiding behind the way she was being happy. He wished that she'd stop.

The garage. It had an old car in it. A gift from her father. Boxes. Shelves. The smell of a garage. He liked that it was tidy.

The living room. All wood too. Wide open. Space to

move around. Big windows. Books. A piano. She turned on a light and the place went sharper. The details. Sky darkening already through the windows. He kept his eyes on the piano while he moved. The light on its body. The white and black keys. His fingers wanting to be on them.

Then the bathroom. 'You know this room already. Paid it a visit or two.'

Leading the way. Only one room left down the hallway.

'And this is the bedroom.' How much did her voice change. When she said that. It softened everything between them. It stripped away the happiness she was faking and showed a little hurt there. He was behind her. She turned to look at him. Uncertain. They were close. She put her hands to his chest. Almost pushing. But not that hard. She looked at his throat. It reminded him of her in the dark. The way her eyes shut. And when they had opened again he saw deeper meaning there. Something tugging in her. Breathlessness. Tugging in him with his eyes fixed on hers. He had been married then. Their first time together. The way the slightest touch had thrilled her. The way she meant it. Almost twenty years. And they were still there. Back in that place. In a strange house. Like at a party. A strange house. Someone else's bedroom.

'It's good to see you.' She said his name. Tears in her eyes. She was thinking of something else. Not him. He was covering something up for her.

He looked at the bed. It was the place he wanted to be least. Not now. It wasn't right. It wouldn't work with whatever was the matter with her. He wouldn't work. Something to do with his heart, they told him. He felt he was dead in that place. That he couldn't please her made him angry. That there was no hope.

Her hands rubbed his chest. She kept looking at his throat. Tipsy. She licked her top lip. Couldn't check his eyes. Didn't want to see his eyes now. Just wanted him. Not like before.

He could do anything. To her. Not with her. It would be to her. Maybe that's what she wanted. To be taken so she'd forget. He took her hands off him. Held them.

'Why are you so cold?' She was worried. The booze made her react. To care more.

'Like what?'

'Your hands.' She put them between hers. They were smaller. She stepped back. Into the bedroom. He wouldn't go. Not in that room where other things had happened. He wouldn't do it. Not to her. Be a part of that. Whatever was in there. Hanging in the air. Perfume covering something up.

'You know, don't you?' Her face was asking him something. Everything in her face. It only made him angrier. He looked around the bedroom. Too much in there. Money spent to pretend. Where it happens should be sweet. Soft. Where it happens should smell nice. Be special. That wasn't love.

'What's the matter?'

He turned away. Ugly. Brutal. Gut-rotten.

Down the hallway. The front door with the pretty coloured glass. His fist wanted to go through. To leave his mark. Stepping to get out. The doorknob in his hand. Twisting. The front door. Opened.

'You can't walk.' She called out his name. 'I'll drive you.'

'It's not that far,' he said. His feet moving.

In between 10 p.m. and 6 a.m. In his house. They wanted the address of where he would be living. That was one of the rules. The conditions of release. While they waited to make certain he was innocent. Waited for someone to approve it. Get around to signing some papers. He waited too. Holes in Grom's testimony. DNA. Who killed the woman? Who killed the woman who had once been his lover? Doreen Stagg. They would never figure it out now. It was all too old. Too far away. Too gone. One of the men he had been with that night. He shut it off. Shut it down. He didn't care. Couldn't care. Was afraid to care. It kept coming back to him. The fun they had been having. Another bottle of rum. How it began to darken. It was enough to be out. Grom.

He shut it off. The dead woman. The victim. He shut it off. Before her name came again. Her face he could almost see. The dead woman he didn't even remember killing. If that's what he did. There had been a visit that night. From him. Doreen Stagg's face. Late at night. It was always something he went to see. With his drunk eyes. Doreen Stagg would be there. Doreen Stagg would be waiting. Others had seen him going in. Blackness to him. The photos he had seen in court. What was left of her. The hairs they found on him. Not the victim's. Same colour. Same length. Not hers. Who did they belong to? He had no idea. DNA could say they weren't the victim's. DNA could not say who owned them. Sit still while it all went away. He hoped. Sit still with Ruth at a distance. A house in the woods. Sit while his wife talked on the telephone. About her plans. He stopped answering the door. Randy could walk right in. That was fine. Randy could do what he liked. Come and go. No one else would walk right in. Maybe a few of his wife's friends. But he ignored them. Like they always ignored him.

He stood from the kitchen table and moved to the living room. His wife left the room with the new cordless phone. Went into the kitchen. She could go anywhere with that. And still talk.

He sat on the couch. Randy was already there.

Watching television. Fingers plugged in his ears. Randy tilted his chin toward where the wife had gone.

He picked up the remote. Checked the channels with the sound down. Nothing. Then his picture came on. He watched the announcer talk.

'Turn it up.' Randy grabbed the remote from him. Turned up the volume. The green notches on the screen going higher. The announcer's voice. Knowing what it was saying. Important by the sound of it. Because it told facts.

Randy watched with a smile. He plucked on his cigarette. 'What're they saying about you now, lover?' Randy looked at him. Proud. He blew smoke out through tight lips.

The announcer said things that he already knew. They kept saying the same things. Every half-hour. On the news channel. He stood up and turned off the television. Randy was looking up at him.

'Sick of yourself,' said Randy.

'Sick to death.' He looked out the window. The one window. Ruth. The one window that showed him the narrow street and a row of houses. He looked around the living room. The pink plastic flowers hanging from a white plastic pot in the corner. The picture of him and his wife with the six kids in the glossy wooden clock. Years ago. More hair. The clothes they were wearing then. All of them alive. She'd taken it from the old house.

That was it. The only thing. The television. New and big. Someone from a group gave it to them. A donation from a store. Other things too. The new telephone. Bags of food. There was talk of a car. A trip to the mainland. To see an all-star hockey game. To go on a shopping spree. All paid for by donations.

People liked that he was out. They liked the idea that the law was wrong. That's what they liked best. Ms. Brophy. She was looking after him. The transition. The Society for the Wrongfully Convicted. She had been visiting him in jail. Someone to talk to. She was convinced of his innocence. Always with those ideas. What could be done. New rules. New regulations. The system changing. There was always more to be done for the wrongfully convicted. Ms. Brophy never gave up. Got him a new lawyer. One who understood. She was on the television too. They talked to her. She had a purpose by the looks of her. She was outraged that things like this could happen. Things like him.

'Let's go for a beer.' Randy with his eyebrows raised. 'You remember beer?' Like it was in a foreign language. He made a motion to lift an imaginary bottle. 'Beer.'

He looked down at Randy. The smoke coming out of him in nicely shaped rings. Watching the rings travel and break apart.

'Why not,' he said. It wasn't a question.

Randy shrugged. 'You got somewhere to go?' Played serious. Then laughed a wheeze. The two front teeth missing. Who liked the looks of that?

In between 10 p.m. and 6 a.m. The thought came to him. Then he shut it off.

He didn't have to take a penny from his pocket. They were always buying him beer. And if they didn't it was Tommy behind the bar. Tommy wouldn't let him pay. Not now. Tommy knew. Tommy had been inside. Tommy had been inside because Tommy confessed. But Tommy had been innocent. This he knew about Tommy. No Society for the Wrongfully Convicted. Not for petty stuff like that. Tommy had gone in for someone else. Someone close to him. Tommy had protected his sister. She had robbed a gas station. Tommy's coat on the camera. His sister had no sense. A big girl. The same size as Tommy. Practically the same name. Tammy. The same hair. Long and curly red. Not anymore. Tommy had his cut short now.

The room was big. Wide open. Wooden floors scuffed black in places. The smell of beer drank for years. Cigarettes fizzled out in beer bottles. Drinkers who drank from morning until dark. Daybreak to blackness coming early. Shutting down the day. The place was just up the street. Around the corner. A woman on a stool. Greasy black hair. Head hanging down. Two men. One to either side of her. Looking out for her. They looked the same. The two men. Waiting to go off. The woman. Blood between them. He knew who they were. Have nothing to do with that family. He kept his eyes off them. Something he'd learned in the pen. Eye contact for no more than a second. The fuse only that long in some.

Another woman. Young one laughing loud. Must be in her twenties. He already knew her. From around. She'd leave with anyone in the place. Back again in fifteen minutes. Looking for another beer. One beer. Out back if you wanted. Made that way. Born defective. Her hands always filthy. Her fingernails black. Ruth in his head. Laughing. Easy. Gentle. The days when they just sat and she thought the world of him. In one restaurant or another. Ruth liked restaurants. She liked walking. Looking at houses. She liked seeing people moving in windows. The marvel of their lives, she had said. He remembered that. She liked crafts. That craft show at the stadium. He had seen how she admired those people. What they could make with their hands. The marvel of their lives. He turned his back on her. Why did he do that? For his family. His children. He had three when he met her. Small ones. Better off without him. He should have left. It made no sense to him now. It didn't back then either. What he was giving up for what. Making children with his wife. Both of them drunk. Always drunk to get there. The reasons. Most of what he did back then was a mystery. He thought about it all. Fourteen years. He thought about it all. But it was still a mystery. It was only the mistake he saw.

Music came from the jukebox. A country and western song. Maybe twenty-five people in the room. He took a swig of beer. The noise of talk got louder than the music. Then wasn't. The music took over. It went up and down. People came and left. But most stayed put. Elbows on the bar.

Randy bought him another beer. Drinking it didn't work the same since he was out. Before it had made him feel better. Most times. Bad sometimes. So bad he became one thing. Only. One emotion. A black-eyed storm. The force brewing in his eyes. Watching out from behind it. One fast action. Release. Noise and flash. Damage done for the sake of calm. After the fact. For the sake of forgiveness. Now it was all bad. It made him see what he was a part of. In the centre of. Left him floating like something rotten in the spill of it.

He took another swig. Drained the bottle. Started on the other. He could rip his own fucking head off. He felt it coming. Randy watched down the bar. Randy's brother was there. He ignored Randy. Always did. Randy looked at him. Then he looked at the glass ashtray. Took up his cigarette. Plucked a draw from it. Another. Then crushed it out. Kept crushing it out.

'Let's go downtown,' Randy said. He laughed. Raised his eyebrows. Coughed. 'We need to go downtown and boogie.' Randy slapped him on the shoulder. 'What say, lover?'

He looked at Tommy behind the bar. Tommy was watching him. Tommy knew what it was about. But Tommy knew more. Tommy owned the bar. Tommy wasn't stupid.

'You off?' Tommy asked.

He shook his head. He finished the other beer. Had another that Tommy laid out for him. He wanted to ask Tommy about his sister. To know what she was up to. He liked the idea that she was big. A big woman. Tall and stocky. Must be six foot two or three. The thought of her made him feel better. But he couldn't mention her name. What would Tommy think to ask it? It would mean something else to Tommy.

Outside. A police car was pulled up across the road. Police lights sweeping around. Officers talking to two boys. One of them ran and the officers didn't go after him. They just looked at the other one. They knew where everyone lived.

He crossed the street with Randy hurrying up behind

him. Randy grabbing at his arm but missing. He passed close to the officers. Right in front of them. Closer than normal. They never bothered to look. He wished they would. Every muscle hard in him.

Down over the hill. Past the graveyard with the trees frozen cold in the winter. Streetlights on the leaves shadowing the names. Big buildings at the bottom of the slope. Downtown. Lots of people around. Friday night by the looks of it. There were bars where they went all their lives. Cheap beer and liquor. Dim and smoky inside. It was hard to make anyone out. They were still open. The people were the same as at Tommy's. Not like the people up on George Street. Younger people up there. People with money. Clothes from magazines. Tourist cafés with local food on the menu. Dishes you tried as a dare. Seal flipper pie. Blueberry grunt. Jiggs dinner. Cod tongues. Dance bars. Bright inside so you could see. Everyone watching faces. Wanting their faces seen. People outside with guitars. People swinging balls of fire on strings at night. People juggling. Faces painted white. Black tears. All of it about money. Fancy begging. Everyone done up to get fucked. He never went there. Stuck to his own bars. The darker ones where the people couldn't talk. He felt he was never like them. So there he was. He was always standing. He never stumbled. He drank and walked out. Perfectly upright. Went somewhere else. Drank and walked out. Nothing could put him down. There was something about the people that he loved. They were heart-mangled. Not just for the moment or the week or month. It was their family legacy. To exist in these places. Something about them that he felt always needed help. He was part of it. He needed help. There was no mystery there. Not anymore. He had lived like that. He thought he loved them because he could see the difference. There was no difference. He was not the strong one. He was just in there. One and the same. They all felt better maybe. Like they were only there for the others. To help. All of them crippled over and crawling. But always someone worse. If he could see what they were really like. Plugged black in the mouth. Like him.

Her number was not listed in the book. The light in the phone booth was useless. Low. He tried to see but his eyes were bad. He called the operator and asked for her number. It wasn't listed. Unlisted. Private.

He said it was an emergency. He told the operator that he was her brother and he had lost her number. He was in from another city. That their mother was dead. Crushed by a falling tree. The first thing that came to mind. He'd been away for years. Nice to be back. But not for this. The operator believed him. He could tell. But she couldn't give him the number. She said she was sorry. Late at night. In a room with other operators. Maybe she was tired. Maybe she was a good person who was doing this. Didn't want it. Didn't like it. A job to pay the bills. He saw that. A human being.

'Do you have the address?' she asked. 'I can give you the address.' She wanted to step through the telephone. Not hide behind it.

Only one Ruth Hawco listed. It must be her.

'Okay.' He accepted the address. He already knew it. But he accepted it from the operator. He was thankful. He thought the operator must be a nice person. Her voice. It was lonely. It was soothing him. He wanted to kiss her. Kiss the face off her. Spin her around in circles. Ballroom music. He thanked her again. He hung up the receiver. Regretted not getting more from her. Her name. Her phone number. If he called back, he'd just get someone else. The booth was right off the sidewalk. People passed by. Couples and groups of three or four. One or two always louder than the others. Trying to make their point. Their point the most important. Everyone should know. They walked quickly.

He picked up the receiver. He found her father's number in the book. Could barely make it out. But made sure it was right. Put it to memory. What time was it? He didn't care. He dialed the number. It rang seven, eight times. He lost count. A man answered. Voice like it had been woken up.

'Hello?'

He listened. A voice that meant business.

'Hello?' A little louder. Curious. This time of night. Almost demanding. Time was money.

He listened.

The voice listened. Ruth's father.

He turned away and looked at the people passing on the street. Young people mostly. Just passing by. Not a care in the world. What did they know? How sorry would they all be one day?

'Hello?'

'Fuck you.'

'Who is this?'

'Fuck you.'

The line clicked on the other end.

He was proud of his vocabulary. What better words. He watched the people pass by. They didn't even see him. They were talking. Words about things that meant nothing. Such-and-such here and there. So-and-so did this or that. Easy to get by at that age. A breeze. Make sure your hair is okay. Your clothes fit or don't. The right smell comes off you. Some of them laughing. A ton of good times out there. All of it useless in the end. No one really listening. No one really giving a shit. Only in it for themselves. Years and years of it. And then what? His arm stiffening. He held the receiver tighter in his fist. The silence on the other end. When he moved, he came away with it.

Look at that house. He stood in the lane. The house was raised from the ground. Built on higher ground. The ocean was not far away. He could smell it in the air. Saltwater. A house in the country. By the sea. The cab cost a bit of money. More than he thought. The silver cord of the receiver hung out of his pocket.

Ruth's house. Who had built it? A man with a beard. A man wearing a sweater. A man who went for walks in the woods. A man who knew the names of things. What had they been thinking to make this house so different? Who did they think they were? In the trees. Dark wood outside. Not painted but stained. Two lights on. One in the living room with the piano. He could only see the ceiling. He was down too low. The other on in the bathroom. Even the bathroom with a big window. He looked at his feet. Rocks. Lots of rocks in the lane. All sizes. Big and small in his fist. All that glass.

He followed a wooden walkway around back. Like a balcony. He knocked on the door. Would she answer? Why should she? He should call out. He should call his name so she knew. Shout out his name. He could almost hear it already. The bellow shaking trees. Nudging the grubs and insects. The woods right behind him. Right over his shoulder across a short yard. Animals in there. Awake and moving. The woods and then water. Waves beneath a cliff on the shore at night. But her voice came soon. Small and sleepy: 'Yes?'

'It's me.'

She opened the door.

He had the receiver to his ear. 'Hello?' he said.

It was her laugh that cleaned him.

The piano seat was hard. Smooth. Level. The keys were there. Long white. Short black. He couldn't play. He used to. In high school they told him he was good at it. A pretty teacher there. She noticed something. There was a place he went to practice. Away from everyone. So they wouldn't see. His fingers connecting. Reading sheet music. Trying to solve the puzzle of the pattern. Something difficult that he enjoyed. Making sounds from symbols. He touched one key. Lightly. Barely a sound. He played at a concert. In the auditorium. His mother there. His father not. His mother there. Always trying. Big sunglasses on at night. Having to hide her eyes. The cut of her mouth. Trying to smile for him. Be proud. She was. She was proud. Music just weakened the heart. Already weak enough. He was good at it though. People had said. His mother trying to convince him.

Ruth came to him with coffee. She laid the mug on the piano. No coaster. Nothing was too good to ruin. She didn't care about things. He liked that about her. Good things, yes, but they were just things. A chip. A dent. A scar. It added character. There was a story to it. That was her. The sorts of things she said. She used to give stuff away. If someone liked something in her apartment she'd give it to them. Take it. No, really. It pleased her. That was when he knew her first. In her apartment downtown. Where they used to stay in mostly. He liked to be alone with her. Listen to her talking about things that made him think. He'd met some of her friends. He never said two words. They didn't know what he was. Not a clue.

Ruth sat on the couch across the way. She didn't know if he could play. He wondered if there was some mention of it years ago. Him playing the piano. Being able to. If there was anyone he would show, it would be her. He understood she wouldn't ask him. She'd just wait.

He pressed one key. One finger. Pianissimo. Softer and softer. Until the lights dimmed. He looked up. Ruth had dimmed them. He often thought of that word. Pianissimo. It came into his head when he'd hear a whisper through bars.

Ruth sat again. She had on a bathrobe. It was white with designs at the sleeves. He could smell coffee. Looked at the mug. He didn't want that. If anything he wanted tea.

'You want a beer?' she asked. 'Instead.'

He shook his head. Kept pressing the one key. Sustaining the rhythm. Plunk. Plunk. Plunk. Middle C. C. C. He'd like to play. See if he could remember.

'Go ahead,' she said.

He stopped. Looked at her face. Sitting there on the couch. Her hair loose around her shoulders. Her hands on her lap.

'What?'

'Play something.'

'Don't know how.'

'Yes, you do. You used to play in high school.'

How did she know? He must have told her after all. It barely surprised him.

One finger. One key.

'How's that?'

'Funny.'

'I wrote that. Took me years.'

'Play something.'

He slid his legs all the way in. Straightened his back. Carefully set his fingers to the keys. Paused. Inched the piano stool in closer. Set his fingers in place again. Threw back his head. And played 'Mary had a Little Lamb.' Frantically.

She was rubbing her face when he looked over. She had been smiling. He saw that when she took her hands away.

'Can you do it with more feeling?' she asked.

'No, with less.'

She leaned forward and took up her mug. Checked the surface of the coffee. 'Are we staying up?' she asked.

He looked over his shoulder. Toward the window. Black. Dark. No streetlights out there. He wondered what time it was. Maybe three or four. His fingertips still on the keys. Both hands. Gently slipping back and forth without pressing. Liking the feeling. The smoothness. He checked there. His fingers caressing the keys.

'We could watch the sunrise on the beach.'

He looked at her. The light in her voice bringing up the memory.

'Remember that?' she asked.

He smiled. Shook his head at how she remembered. There was always the good for her to see. Whatever he had been through. Whatever she had been through. She was delicate and stood watching what was small. What things were made of. The design of them. She touched clothes. Felt them with her fingers. Smelled things. That was how she shopped.

He put one finger in his coffee. He blocked his mouth and nose with his other hand. He blew hard until his cheeks puffed out. His eyes scrunched shut. Then he stopped and looked into the mug.

'That's how you make coffee boil,' he said.

She was almost laughing. Her smile was big.

'My granddaughter thinks that's funny.'

'Did you make that up?'

'Yes. I make everything up. Even you.'

The way she looked at him. He knew what she was thinking. The smile going away. He could have been something. She was thinking. He could have amounted to something. Instead of what he was. What he had made of his life. What he had done. Prison. And that woman. Did he really kill that woman?

He stood from the piano. Pulled shut the lid over the keys when he stood. Maybe too hard. The noise told him that. The living room was big. Why did she need so much space? He went right up to a painting. One of the ocean. But the water was orange and pink. Swirling. Maybe it wasn't water at all. How the hell would he know? Why did people waste their time doing things like that? And other people bought them. Like a secret. They were sharing. How clever. A secret that left other people out.

He looked hard to the side. His hands in his pockets. He saw another painting. A woman. He liked that one.

He could see things in it. Tears came to his eyes. Why the fucking tears? He smeared them away with the butt of his palm. He saw himself hunched over. Weeping into his hands. Bawling. His back shuddering. Hunched over like that he would be smaller.

'What's the matter?' Her quiet voice behind him. Soft. Perfect. A hand on his shoulder.

He looked at her and saw that she was watching the painting. Her feet were bare. Bare on a wooden floor.

'Do you know why I bought that one?'

He didn't answer.

She looked at him. Mercy. 'Because she reminded me of your mother.'

Hands to his face. Both hands to his face. He sobbed into them in front of her.

They had missed the sunrise because he had fallen asleep. When he woke it was light. It came without him knowing. He never slept like that. He was in her bed. In her bedroom. He had become a part of it. He tossed back the covers and sat up. She wasn't in the room. He smelled food. Toast. Hushed to sleep like a baby. By her. He remembered. That was okay but sad too. He looked around the bedroom. Big art on the walls. Old furniture. A dresser with fancy brass loops on the drawers. Another piece with three tall mirrors and a stool to sit on. There were combs and brushes. Bottles of cream. Lotion. Hairbands. He stood and went to the dresser. He put his fingers here and there. He opened an old jewelry box. Earrings. Chains. Pins. They probably all had meanings. He thought of taking something. Looked toward the doorway. His heart speeding a little. No one there. He picked up a jar of cream. Screwed the lid off. He smelled it. Shut his eyes. There was nothing but that smell. It could only be her. Found here.

The kitchen was where she was sitting. In that booth. She was watching out the window. She hadn't heard him coming. He just watched her. The same thing every day out that window. He stepped a little nearer. She turned and saw him. She looked at his face. His hair. He looked away. Remembering last night. The living room off the kitchen. The piano.

'What'll happen now?'

'With what?' He stepped toward the stove. Looked at the cast-iron frying pan.

'I read in the paper. You're supposed to be home. One of the conditions, wasn't it?'

'Who says I'm not home?' He thought it best to smile. It might have been the wrong thing to say. Though he didn't look at her. He touched the toaster. It was warm. Maybe what he'd said was too much. Home. He shouldn't have said that about this place. It was hers.

'You want some toast?'

'Sure.' He backed away when she came near. Let her get the bread from the package. Put it in the toaster slot.

'Will they make you go back?'

He waited. Decided on something but didn't say it. Said instead: 'Who knows.'

'I know what you were going to say.'

'Yeah.'

'You're always going back.'

'You think you're so fucking smart.' It wasn't meant to be said that way.

'Not fucking. Just smart.'

She knew how to take him. That was the joy. There was nothing he could really do to hurt her. Except leave. That wasn't what it used to be either. He'd already done that.

The car rolled along smoothly. The bumps were hardly felt. The sway of the vehicle impressive. A few blocks away he said: 'Right here's good.'

She pulled over. Checked the rearview. 'You could've just stayed with me.'

'That's no good for you.'

'Who says?'

He still hadn't asked her about the baby. She hadn't told him. He didn't know why he thought of it then. Something about her. The way she was looking at him.

'I'll see you.'

She took his arm. 'You have my number now.'

One last look at her. He stepped out.

'No need to punish telephones.'

He ducked in for another look. To see that smile he knew would be there. His eyes searching past her. Through her window. Someone from the neighbourhood he might know. A man passing. He didn't recognize him.

'We could go on a proper date.'

His eyes went to her. She had leather gloves on her hands. Brown and skintight. Driving gloves. He felt like an oddity. That was the word.

'I haven't eaten popcorn in a while,' he said.

'You're suggesting a movie?'

'Yeah.'

'Okay.'

He ducked out.

'Hey?'

He ducked back in.

'Thanks for the piano recital last night. Even if it wasn't at the piano.'

For some reason a chill went up his spine. Gooseflesh prickling the hairs on his arms.

'Yeah.' He nodded.

'You know what I mean?'

He didn't say anything. His eyes watching her. His eyes saying: You're so beautiful. Then he said it out loud. It sounded different from his mouth. He ducked out and slammed the door. Too hard maybe. He didn't know. Trying to make a point. It came out wrong. He had to cross the street before she would drive away.

A bunch of people had called. His wife told them he was sick. In bed. The flu. Throat gone.

'You better sound like this.' She pretended to talk in a hoarse voice. Randy had done it. Filled in for him. Randy was there. He raised his beer bottle.

'Hello,' he said with a hoarse voice. 'I'm you this morning.' He laughed. Coughed. The kitchen full of blue smoke.

'Be my guest.'

His wife looked at him. Randy looked at him. He noticed he was smiling.

'What's up with you?' she asked.

He wouldn't give her the time of day. Not now. She wouldn't ruin it for him. She didn't even care where he was. In a bar she probably thought. It wasn't important. As long as he came home before he got his big fat cheque.

'Bobby's getting out tomorrow.' She grinned like she was poking him.

That was it. That was all it took. They would know. The microphones and cameras. They would know about Bobby. They could access records. They made a living digging things up. Drooling over it. Grave robbers.

He thought of Bobby in the corridors. Passing him. Two of them on different units. They'd just nod at each other. Not his place to say a word.

'We got to pick him up.'

Back to that place. Up at eight. Breakfast on the unit. Work in the kitchen. Recreation in the yard. Lunch on the unit. Unit lockdown until two. Afternoon recreation. Carpentry. Weight room. Supper in the unit. Unit lockdown until lights out. In his cell then. From eleven-thirty to eight. Darkness with flashlight checks on the hour. Official count every hour and a half. The machine kept going so you couldn't sleep. Making sure you were there. Headlights across a window at night. It was them.

Bobby released. He'd never get out. He was stupid. The boy was stupid. Eighteen. The baby of the family. Wanting to be the oldest.

He rubbed his face. Tried to forget. Shut down the world just for a second. But it wouldn't work. This was family.

His wife left the kitchen. He felt harder than a moment

ago. But it was only him trying. He felt softer was how it was. He heard her on the telephone in the living room. Something about someone owing someone money. There was a new refrigerator in front of him. White as anything. He didn't realize until he went for the handle and it wasn't in the exact place. The door came open easily. It was bright inside. Two bulbs. Not one. It hummed smoothly. There was food on every shelf. Food in cartons he'd never seen before. Food he would never buy.

'Completely stocked.'

He looked at Randy.

'Delivered that way,' Randy said. 'By very decent people, I might add.' Laughing the way he did. It was nothing but a joke. Everything to him. 'You weren't here, so they said a prayer around the fridge instead.'

Bobby rubbed his hands together in the back seat. Ms. Brophy driving the car. She had just showed up this morning. She was wearing a pin. A colour that meant she cared for the wrongfully convicted. Showed up at the house. The cameras and microphones with her. Attached to her. Who invited her? He had no idea. You need a drive, she had said. She had a car. They didn't have a car. Although his wife kept telling him there were rumours of one.

Him in the front. His wife in the back. A clipboard

between his seat and Ms. Brophy's. Bobby's name on it. Information.

He tried not to look at the wall. The door that buzzed. It was there at his right. Through the window. Pulling at his eyes so he had to look. The high walls. The yard. The corridors. The unit. The cell. The bed.

Cameras and microphones surrounded the car. Human beings, he was thinking while he watched them.

His wife hugged Bobby.

'Hey, Mom,' said Bobby. Like he'd just seen her yesterday. Like there was nothing to it. Inside. Outside. No difference. This was just a bit of it. A bit of fun before it changed again.

'Where to?' asked Ms. Brophy. The car not moving. The faces in all the windows. Mister Myrden. Who did they want this time? Him or his son. Mister Myrden.

Bobby leaned between the front seats.

He turned to look at his son. Face like his father's.

Bobby was watching Ms. Brophy's face.

'Who're you?' he asked.

'I'm from the Society for the Wrongfully Convicted.'

'Yeah.' Bobby stared at her. His eyes flooding with darkness. 'That's your fucking name?'

His wife snickered.

'Watch your language,' he said.

'Friends in fair weather,' said Bobby. Falling back into his seat.

That was smart, he thought.

The cameras and microphones stayed near. Tapping on the glass. Talking. Even with no one answering. Talking anyway. All sound muddled. Mister Myrden. There was nowhere he could look without seeing one. Wanting in.

Ms. Brophy just stayed there. She wasn't in a hurry. Pretending that she was deciding.

He looked at her. 'Drive the car,' he said.

She did it right away. Clicked the transmission stick. Started edging away from the prison lot. The microphones and cameras not wanting to get out of the way. Moving so they could still be there and not get crushed. The car went ahead. They moved out of the way. Had to. Those human beings with their breakable parts. All behind them. Watching the car go. Gone. They were quiet then. Stood there. Sad. Watching the car pull away. Not knowing what to do. The end of the world.

He looked at the back seat. His wife and Bobby watching out the back window. The microphones and cameras shrinking away. He looked at Ms. Brophy. Her eyes on the rearview. What put her in this place? There was always something. Driving criminals around.

Dangerous people. With no concern. Who did she think she was? Who was she trying to save? In the missionary position.

He tried talking to Bobby. Bobby wasn't listening. Bobby had a plan in his head. He was eighteen. Lots of movement. Schemes already set up. Crime was nothing but a laugh. With no one dead yet. There were people he needed to see. Those who had kept visiting. Prison not bothering them. His buddies. Locked inside. A medal. A woman. To polish the medal. Robin was her name. Bobby was good to her. Women liked Bobby. He never laid a finger on them. Plans and action. Lots of action. His body wanted it. To move around. That was all. He hadn't been in long enough to go deeper than that. It was all still anger with him. He was going to show them. Take what he could get.

Fourteen years you get past those plans. You lose your plans. People make plans for you. You become almost nothing. Nothing to no one. People forget about you. You forget. You disappear. Up at eight. Lights out eleven-thirty.

'New fridge,' said Bobby. He ate whatever was near. In a hurry. Took a piece of roast pork. Ate it. Drank milk from the carton.

'Use a glass,' said his wife. Going to the cupboard and

-90-

bringing one down. She held it out. Bobby never took it. Never looked at her. She laid the glass on the counter. Banged it down and left the room. The TV on. Then the telephone. Both of them at once. Volume up.

Bobby folded the top of the milk carton. Put it back in the fridge. He shut the door. Looked at him.

'You're going back in,' he said to his son. In the past, he wouldn't have said a word. Thinking it wasn't his place. Let them live. Let them learn.

Bobby shook his head. 'No fucking way.' He moved his shoulders. Tilted his head one way. Stiff from lying down. Stiff from standing up. One place all the time. Staring. Planning. Caged on the unit. Caged with other men. A sore neck from holding your head up.

'You'll put yourself back in there.'

'You believe that.'

'I don't believe it. You'll do it.'

'Ah, I don't care.'

He stood from his chair and Bobby went still.

'You don't care?'

Bobby said nothing. Watched the floor. His shoulders going down a little. 'What's to do?' His voice like a little boy's.

The question shut off his voice. He said: 'Get a job.'

'Get a job!' Bobby looked at him. Nervous in his eyes. 'What's that?'

He took a step nearer. Fool, he thought. He didn't like it. The sound of Bobby's voice. Stupid boy.

'Sure, you're rich. What'd I need a job for?' He was snarky-looking now. Disrespectful. 'Look at you. Wrongfully accused. I saw it on TV.' He tried smiling but it was jumpy. 'Look at me. Wrongfully accused. Me too.' He put both hands to his own chest. But blaming someone else. Pushing against someone else. He looked weak when he did that. He was standing in one spot. No fidgeting anymore. He'd stopped. 'Me too.'

And that was it. The boy was gone. Like that. Out the door. Banged shut. The cameras and microphones meeting him there again. Bobby stopping to make a speech about being wrongfully accused.

He felt sick. He stepped closer to the door so he could hear it. Make himself sicker. He stood near the door and saw the blur of movement through the blurry glass.

'How do you mean, wrongfully accused?' one of them shouted.

'Runs in the family,' said Bobby.

A few laughed. Others didn't know what that meant. It stumped the hell out of them.

He took his wallet out from his back pocket. They had given it to him when he got out. He opened it and had a look. His expired driver's license. His hospital card. A photograph of his daughter. Jackie was still in school then. She looked like Caroline. They could be one and the same. This wallet had been his father's. The only thing he had of him. His father had died in prison. Who knew why. There had been an investigation. But no one knew anything more after. He had picked up the envelope. Just the wallet inside. That was all. And the wedding ring from the morgue. He kept it in the wallet. The imprint cut into leather. Showing through.

The microphones and cameras were there the next morning. He heard them outside the door. More than usual. The sound telling him something wasn't right. More chaos. The more chaos the more of them. Maggots and stink.

He wouldn't open the door because it would all come at him. Be let loose. He stood there. The blurry glass with the moving blur. Everyone like one changing clump. A painting from Ruth's house.

'What's going on?' his wife asked. He looked over his shoulder. She was up on the stairs. Just out of bed.

'Don't know.'

Bobby Myrden. He heard the name. The telephone rang. It couldn't be seven in the morning. His wife ran back into the bedroom. The telephone. She said hello and she already knew.

Bobby Myrden. More voices outside the door. More of them gathering. Bobby Myrden.

Silence upstairs. Not a sound. Then what he took for a sob. Strange coming from his wife.

The questions never ended. He kept thinking of them. His heart filled up with 'why' and 'if only.' He couldn't breathe at times. There was no answering. Carrying a casket. The pain in his chest. It was heavy. He was tired enough to drop. No strength. What was inside. Questions all around. Trouble swallowing. Where to shift his eyes. Carrying a casket. The weight in there. With five other men. His three sons and his brothers. One of his sons home from the mainland. Mac in a long black coat. White shirt. Black tie. White gloves. The only one who had made it out. The eldest. The owner of a factory that made eyeglasses. Didn't touch a drop. Gave it up. Straightened out. Now, holding the casket too.

His second dead son. First Chris and now Bobby. Chris. Twenty-three years old. Skinny little Chris. Not dead in a car crash like that reporter had said. Her facts wrong. Only the girlfriend dead. Chris beaten to death in an alleyway days later. No witnesses. Buried him deep.

The graveyard. A crowd in the bitter air. All of them

in coats. Their eyes not wanting any part of this. They had to be there. They had to stand and watch. One good turn deserved another. Relatives. They had to bear it. A comfort to the living. The cameras and microphones. Trying to be quiet. Trying to pretend they weren't there. Be invisible.

Ruth. He could look at her for a second. That was it. She knew where he was.

His wife on one side of him. Jackie on the other. He stood there staring at the shiny box. The only place his eyes could go now. The polished wood. The handles for lifting. Resting there over the hole. The priest talking. Words that meant nothing. He sniffed and wiped at his nose. The white gloves the funeral man had given him. They were thin. No good against the cold.

The priest was finished. He shut the book he was reading from. He looked at the casket. A time of joy, he had said. Celebration. But his eyes weren't filled with that. He knew what it all really meant. We will be together. We will be welcomed to a better place. We will be safe in the arms of Jesus.

Who knew what to do now? No one dared move.

A man from the funeral home leaned and pressed a button. The box went down. Slow and steady. That was the hardest part. His knees going weak. Jesus wasn't in the earth. With the damp blackness and bugs. Jesus wasn't there. Jackie took hold of his hand. She let herself. She let herself take hold of his hand. A shudder in his chest. His daughter touching him. Christ almighty. Fucking Christ almighty. His head bowed more. His hand in hers. Her warm fingers through his thin white glove. Holding on like when she was small. She gave his hand a little squeeze. That's all it took. Tears pouring down his cheeks. Jackie. I'm so sorry.

Mac had just turned and walked away. Back into his big black rental and gone. A hug for his mother first. No words. That was it. Who knew where he went then? Was he in a hotel? Was he gone on a plane? He was his own man. Relatives had wished him well. He would say nothing to his brothers. A quiet word or two to Jackie. Mac had kissed her on the cheek. One look at him. One quick look at him with those eyes. Then gone. Away from here.

His sons were singing around midnight. In the kitchen. His brothers singing too. Their voices like one in his chest. They never came together like this. Everything was peaceful. Everything was okay. To have them there. Except for the emptiness. How Bobby had died. The rumours. It could have been anyone. Who did this. Who died. He tried not to remember. Bobby as a boy. Bobby as a man who made his choices. That was easier to face.

Blame who? It never helped. He'd learned that. Been taught that. Blame yourself.

The people all stood around. Against the kitchen counter. In the kitchen doorway. Bottles and glasses in their hands. All of them there. They couldn't fill the space of one missing. He just noticed. Everyone gone quiet now. Except his sons. They were singing ballads that he used to sing. Ballads his father used to sing. Their voices. His heart was so full of it. Full of love for them all. He took another mouthful of rum. Beer was not good enough for this. Shut his eyes. Tried to believe in it. Waited. Listening for when the harmony of their voices stopped. When he stopped singing. And then there was a woman's voice. The part where the woman came in. Jackie's voice. Sweet as an angel's. Steady and true. In sadness. She was even there. Singing for Bobby. The tone of her voice all full of Bobby. Stilling every bit of movement. Stilling every thought in every head. Only pure emotion in the heart now. Overcome.

Caroline still up too. On his lap. Quiet as anything. One arm around her belly. Him holding her while she listened to the voices. While her eyes watched her mom sing. Her uncles join in again. Her small sweet face just watching. Her mouth open a little. Sweet lips. Sweet cheeks. Eyes full of wonder. Nothing like this she'd ever seen before. Up this late with relatives. What did any of it mean?

Chapter Three

It was hard to lift his head from the pillow. Not one thing mattered. Not one person. He didn't care if the days kept moving by. Without him. His eyes felt burned out. His lids. Ashes over lead. They stared at the carpet until he shut them.

He'd slip away. A dream of his children. Each of their names tattooed on his back. Someone digging in there. Into his flesh. Notches to be crossed off. Where he was the killer. They were buried in places only he knew. Under a big area of earth without grass. Dug up and then trampled. A police detective was asking him. The police detective knew everything. Then he'd wake to the sound of the telephone or someone banging on the front door. It was like he was buried in mud. Only his face showing.

Who was he kidding? he kept asking himself. His bones were dead weight. His limbs good for nothing. It was only the machinery in his body that kept him alive. The heartbeat that he'd wish would finally shut down. It didn't know when to quit.

He thought of Ruth. In her house. Alone. The thought like grey stone. Caroline. Jackie. Grey boulders. Willis. The rumours of how Bobby died. Willis and Grom. It made him heavier to think. It stitched him to the bed.

He opened his eyes. The same. Nothing different. Every single thing, every single person, exactly the same. The same weight. The same colour. The same worthless meaning. What did he have to do with any of them? If they all died, he wouldn't know how to care. It'd only help him sleep better, darker, deeper. Their deaths. Gather them up like stones in his arms. And jump over the edge. Into nothing.

Days later Randy came in and sat on the bed. 'You better yet?' He rocked the bed a little. Testing it. 'Good springs. I could use a nice mattress like this.' He glanced toward the doorway. Checking. Like there was a secret to be told. Then whispering: 'Come on, get up. So I can haul it over to my place. How's the box spring?'

He stared at the ceiling, one arm heavy across his forehead. In and out of focus.

'Got a cold?' Randy made to check his forehead for fever.

He slapped the hand away. It just happened. He didn't even mean to do it. No feeling in his skin.

Randy stood, but he took no offense. 'Come on, rise

and shine.' He knocked the edge of the bed with his knees. 'Up, lazy head. Time for school.'

He said nothing.

Randy just stood there, breathing. He swallowed. Looked around the room. 'You better come stay with me for a while. No one here to pamper ya.'

He sighed just to breathe.

Randy went to the closet. He pulled out an old suitcase and opened it on the bed. He stood facing the closet. 'You want some of these dresses?'

He turned his head away.

'I wouldn't mind a few,' said Randy. 'Yes, here's just the one. Yellow suits my complexion. I've been told as much. Wait a second. That was before a fight.'

Tears in his eyes. That's all humour could get out of him. They weren't even his tears. They weren't even a part of him. They just came. Like they thought they might be laughter.

He was drinking in a bar. The last time he looked at the clock it was after three in the morning. The door locked. People pounding on it to get in. There was no one he wanted to see. He kept drinking. That was enough to occupy him. That was all he wanted to do with his life. Drink rum and be sure of himself. Sure of the sameness of him and the rum. Only barely in the world then.

Randy was gone off or somewhere else in the bar.

It was dark all around him. His hand on the glass. Trying not to think. He didn't bother to look up. His arms on the bar ledge. Staring down into his drink. Not listening. Not hearing. Drink.

'Look at who it is.' A voice too close behind him.

He knew the voice. The door closing. The echo of it. How long ago was that? The sound just in his ears. Not sinking deeper. The way booze helped that happen.

Fat voice, full of gravel, getting closer. 'It's Mister Innocent in the flesh.'

He didn't need to turn around. It was Grom. Grom and who else? Willis. Maybe two or three others. The more the merrier.

Grom came up beside him. Stared up at his face. Breathing heavy because he always did. All that fat around his throat. Plus, he was drunk. 'Mister Innocent. How 'bout a drink, wid all your innocent money?'

He kept staring into his drink. The coils tightening in his shoulders and arms, in his stomach and jaw. If they wound too tight it would be over for all of them. A roar would leap out as he spun around. A flash and no one left standing. Every worthless person snapped in so many places.

Grom laid a fat hand on the bar, fingers stuffed shiny. 'Rum,' he called to the bartender.

When the bartender delivered the glass, Grom said to her: 'Mister Innocent's paying.'

The bartender looked at him.

He stared at her. Face never changing. Not now. Not ever.

'I don't think so,' she said to Grom, smiling in a twisted way that said she didn't like Grom.

'I think he is.' Grom swallowed his drink. 'And he'll pay fer 'nother too.' The empty glass went down on the bar. Smack. Grom was in need of another, but Grom was in control.

The bartender looked at him again. She glanced at the space between him and Grom, at the men that were there. How many. Her eyes shifted. From one to the other. Two more. Standing in wait.

'You wan' the truth. Pay for it. Pay.' Fat finger pointed. Into the hollow of Grom's glass.

He raised his full glass and took a quiet drink. Looking straight ahead. He tasted the rum. It was sweet. Pleasant. No burn left in it. Everything to the sides of him. Staying that way. He was a patient man.

Grom leaned nearer, said in a voice he tried to make low: 'Doreen Stagg. Who'd fun wid Doreen Stagg?' He gave a laugh, his mouth held open. 'Ha. Who? Ha ha.' Leaning back. Away. Fat palm slapping the bar. Nearly missing. Good one.

His body might go off at the slightest touch. A fingertip. A breath of air.

Grom looked back at the two behind him.

'Give him another,' he said.

The bartender poured another. Grom's glass filling up. Her eyes not sure what was coming next. It would be difficult. Whatever it was.

'Nice.' Grom drank it back. 'What 'bout the boys?'

'All of them,' he said to the bartender.

They were to all sides of him in a second. Grom on his right. Squid and Willis on his left. Elbows on the bar. Everyone drinking rum that he paid for. Cozy little group of pals. One of them a murderer. Several times over.

'Like old times,' Grom said, raising his glass.

The others raised their glasses.

'Old times,' he heard Willis say. Laughing with danger in it. The danger of everything tied to him. Caroline and Jackie.

Forget them.

He kept silent. Tried not to think. He'd been able to keep them out of his head. Let them live their lives. Without him. He was free. The booze was just good enough. But now there was Willis. Who was free now.

He noticed Grom watching his face. Waiting to say something. Wanting to get it out of his system. Grom's eyes kept checking him over.

The silence was more than he wanted to take. The mangling silence wanted to get out. Spread itself around. Him between these three men who knew more about him than he did. That night. They were there. All of them. Maybe others too.

And what about Bobby?

It was only a matter of who would die now. Who was next.

Grom kept staring. The fat grin on his fat face.

It was hard to keep his eyes from going there. From looking to see what Grom was really after. What he had to say. What sort of injury was intended. Then he said what he had been saving up. Just for such an occasion. Maybe saving it for days: 'Sorry about your boy.'

The bartender stopped. Squid and Willis too. Never moved another muscle. The sound behind him dropped away. Life gave up.

Sorry about your boy.

Boy.

It hit him. It shook him. Not just the death, but the way Grom said it. The apology. The way the words were shaped. The way they told him that Grom was a part of it. He turned his head and looked at Grom's face. The rum in his eyes spoke. Explained everything.

His hands shot out. Grabbed hold of Grom. His fingers dug into his own palms through Grom's bunched-up shirt. He raised his fist. But Grom was gone. Yanked away. Straight to the right. Just like that. He turned to hear the thud-cracking of a fist against skin. Randy there. Belting Grom three times in the face. Hard. Fast. Randy's face screwed up the way it was when he was the angriest he could be. Nose squat higher. Teeth showing like a rat's. Elbow far back. Three quick, spring-loaded rock-hard smacks. And Grom dropped where he was. Rolled a little. All that flesh. Wobbling. Then Randy came after Squid with both hands. Yanked him out into clear space and hit him with his elbow. One, two, three. That's all it took. Squid blind on his feet. Randy snatched up a bottle and crashed it off Squid's chin. The smell of beer in the air. Glass dust on Randy's face. He grabbed up an old-timer's cane and swung it. It swept through the air. The magical swoosh. A sound from playing superheroes as a boy.

'Randy,' the bartender shouted. Everyone knew she liked Squid. Had a thing for him. 'Randy, stop.' She came out from behind the bar. 'Randy! I'm fucking warning you.' Made a move to get near Randy. But flinched back when a gob of blood struck her blouse. She looked at the shadows sitting at the tables. No one cared enough to move.

Willis knew he was next. He swallowed the rum in his mouth and hurried to get by Randy while Squid's face took the final cane smack. Randy tossed away the weapon just as Squid crumbled to the floor. He swung around and hit Willis while he was moving. One punch was all that it took to knock Willis's feet out from under him. Sweep his legs into the air and send him crashing back over a table and chairs. One smack because Willis was moving forward at the same time. He should have known better than to race ahead like that. It might have saved his nose, because it snapped. Everyone could hear it let go. That sound hurt everyone within hearing distance.

Randy picked up a chair and finished the job. Nothing but a single chair leg left in his hand when he was done. Splinters made of everything. Then he stood there in his jean jacket and jeans. Thin but solid. He dropped the chair leg. He brushed back his hair with the flat of his palm. Not even breathing heavy. He dusted off his jean jacket. Gave a that-was-nothing smile. Then his eyes caught sight of Grom moving a little. Groaning.

'What a fucking insult.' Randy swung back his leg and kicked until Grom stopped. The lace on his steel-toed boot slapping around. Come undone. He lifted his boot onto a chair and tied up the two ends. A perfect bow.

'You okay?' Randy asked him, wandering over. He tilted his head and winked. 'They didn't hurt ya, did they?'

He frowned. Shook his head. Watched a few people

staggering out. Leaving. The show over. Door opened. Door closed.

'I nearly broke out in a sweat there.' Randy laughed when he said that. Even before he was done. Almost nervous.

The bartender was bent down next to Squid. She was shaking him. Saying his name. But he wouldn't wake up.

'Look,' she said to Randy. Misery holding misery. 'Look.'

'I'm looking,' said Randy. 'Looks good.' Only his voice in the dead-quiet room.

All of this made him feel better. Relaxed his muscles. Like he'd had a good night's sleep, or a massage. The one Ruth gave him one night. Her fingers into his flesh. Loosening him. Prying him away from himself until he dropped off. All the trouble gone out of him.

The bartender moved back behind the bar. She was angry. Stomping. A savage woman on a mission. Going for something.

'I'm thirsty,' said Randy, stepping up to the bar. He reached for Grom's glass. Raised it. Looked at it. Waited a second. Swirled it around. Sniffed it. Then shot it back. 'Booze's a miraculous germ killer.'

The sound of a receiver slammed down behind the bar. He turned to see the bartender. Done with her call. Arms folded across her chest. Just you wait.

'Who you think she called?' Randy asked.

He finished off his drink. Not in a big hurry, but knowing it was time to go.

'Maybe she was just checking her lotto numbers.' Then something came over Randy. A wave of pain shutting off his smile. 'Yee-ouch.' He raised his right hand. Like it'd been electrocuted. Shook it. Made a fist as best he could. Looked at his busted knuckles. 'Merciful Christ!' Then to him: 'Can you believe that? The way those cruel faces attacked my hand? Poor old hand didn't have a chance.'

It was less than an hour later when they took Randy away.

They were walking up Water Street. Looking at the big boats tied up in the harbour. Planning to climb aboard one and let it take them wherever. Randy was laughing about it. The lives they could lead on foreign shores. 'If only someone'd exile me,' he said. He knew where the boats were from by the names. He knew some of the sailors on each boat. Drank with them. Listened to their stories. Taught them English. Learned bits of French or Portuguese. Bought strange-smelling cigarettes off them. By the carton. Bottles with peculiar labels. Interesting to look at. Laughed at the way everything sounded so different. The way he made a mess of pronouncing things.

A miracle, Randy sometimes said. The way language works.

'Cuba,' he was shouting. Fists up in the air. Over his head. 'Portugal. Take me. I surrender.' Laughing.

Then the lights came on. Red and blue. Washing over them. They just stood there. Every thought of escape knocked out of them like breath.

Randy looked at his feet. 'You got legs?'

'I'm too old to run.'

Randy put his hands in his pockets. Began whistling. Rocking on his heels. There were sparkles on Randy's face. Dust from the smashed beer bottle. A spray of skin-tightening liquid.

The two uniforms came out of their car doors at the same time. One man. One woman. The woman was more anxious than the man. The way she touched her door with one hand. Touched her gun holster with the other. The man didn't touch his holster. He was big. Walked forward without a care in the world. Big boots. Big arms dangling by his sides. He knew what was going on. He'd been there many times. The woman checked her hat. Gave it a tug. The man wasn't wearing one. His hair was combed nicely. Recently clipped. Gelled.

'Evening,' Randy said to them.

The red and blue lights did strange things to their black uniforms. It made piano music play in his head. It swelled up in him. Until his lips were moving and his tongue was quietly stirring the notes around.

Randy looked at him to see what was up.

'What are you two into tonight?' asked the man.

'Out for a stroll,' said Randy. He looked up at the sky. 'Beautiful night. Stars aplenty.'

'Could we see some identification, please?' asked the woman.

Randy patted the front of his shirt. Made a face like he didn't know what that might mean. Identification? Not a clue.

The man looked at Randy's hands. His eyes staying on the swollen, bloodstained knuckles.

He reached behind and pulled out his wallet. Handed it to the woman. As soon as it was in her hand, she held it out to him. Wanting to give it back.

'Take out a piece of identification for me, please, sir.'

He took the wallet and opened it. He didn't know what to give her. His expired driver's license. He plucked it out and gave it over. The license brought Bobby to mind. The things that had been given to them by the police. From the boy's pockets. Teaching Bobby to drive. Skinny little Chris. Always afraid of cars. Police and belongings. The lethal seep. He shut it down.

The woman read the card. Studied it a while. Then said: 'This is expired.'

What's the answer to that? he wondered.

'Does the man look like he's driving,' Randy laughed. 'Fuck sakes.'

'I don't drive anymore.'

Randy laughed again. 'Wouldn't blame ya. Maniacs on the road.' He looked toward the police car. 'Shame you're expired though.' He shook his head once. 'Jesus.' Serious as anything, but licking his lips. Edgy. 'And I thought you were a right lively fellow.'

'Do you have anything that's not expired?'

Randy moved ahead, pointed: 'That's the man's picture there. He hasn't changed that much.'

The woman took offense. Randy moving like that when he wasn't told to.

'Relax,' she said.

The way she said it made him smile. Not really a smile, but something close to it.

Randy said: 'You've put on a few pounds, though. Few wrinkles, too. Next time you're picking up groceries, try shopping in the "wrinkle-free" food section.' He held up his hands. Like he wanted nothing more to do with it. 'My advice only.' A laugh. Looking around to see who was laughing too. No one. He kept fidgeting. Couldn't stay still.

The man took the driver's license from the woman. He looked at it. Then handed it back. 'That's fine, Mister Myrden,' he said. 'How about you?' he asked Randy.

'I don't carry any. I've got no confusion of that sort.'

'What sort?'

'You're the fellow with the uniform. Dressing up. Where's your ID?'

'What's your name?'

'Pablo.' He gestured back to one of the ships.

The man smiled a little. A smile that was in control. He didn't seem bothered by it. The woman looked up at the man to check what was supposed to happen.

'Pablo,' said the man. 'Pablo what?'

'Pablo Picasso.'

'Right,' said the man.

'I have come a long way to paint cubes.' That said with an accent. 'Look at your head.' A few imaginary brush strokes in the air. 'You see. My work here is done.'

The man and the woman watched him.

'Is your name Randy Murphy?'

'No, but that fucker owes me money.'

He chuckled and the woman looked up at him.

The man even gave another smile.

'Do you know this man's name?' the woman asked him.

'He doesn't know a thing,' Randy said. 'It's our first date.'

The man looked at him. 'Mister Myrden,' he said.

He stared at the policeman. Noticed that a few late-night people had stopped to watch what was happening. A show of sorts. The police playing their part. Pass around a hat, he thought. Then he lowered his eyes.

'You'll have to come with us,' said the man.

When he looked up, he saw that the man was talking to Randy.

He stepped closer to Randy. If Randy was in it. Then he was in it too.

'There's no need,' said the man. Holding up a big palm. 'We don't need to talk with you, Mister Myrden. Not right now.'

Randy shrugged. 'Guess you're innocent after all.' Randy let the man take his arm. Let the man lead him away. It was all a joke. He frowned and shrugged again. Then laughed. 'Call my liar,' he shouted back. 'Tell him I've been abducted by aliens. Ugly fucking aliens.'

He followed after Randy. But the woman put up a hand. 'Please, sir,' she said. 'Keep back.' Her other hand went to her stick. Not her gun. She'd only hit him. Not shoot him. That wouldn't be too bad. He could live with that. Break her wrist taking it away from her.

The man led Randy to the car. Took out his cuffs.

The woman stayed there. Looking up at him. Holding that small hand up. No rings on her long fingers. It was a clean hand. Pink. Fragile. He thought he smelled perfume off it. Lotion.

'Hey,' Randy called out.

He looked toward Randy and saw him reach into his pocket. The man grabbed him tighter. The cuffs in one hand. Turned him sideways to face the car. Randy still managed to pull out what he was after and quickly toss it to him.

A ring of keys rattling through the air in a high arc.

He raised his hand and caught it. He knew what the keys were. He didn't need to look. He just held them in his fist.

The woman took some interest in his fist. Thought it might be evidence maybe. Then glanced at his face before turning and walking away. She checked over her shoulder to see that he stayed put. Her hand still on her stick.

The man leaned Randy against the car. He put the cuffs on. There was no fight. No point. None of it mattered.

Randy just laughed and shook his head. How could he possibly be at fault? He'd get out of this. A minor obstacle. When he was in the back seat and the two front doors were shut, the red and blue lights were switched off. The car stayed there for a while. The man talking on his radio. He could see Randy in the back seat. Staring ahead through the wire mesh. He heard Randy singing at the top of his lungs. The words from a country and western song. But the words changed around. So they'd be funny. Wanting to make those two officers laugh.

The man laid down his radio. He was saying something to the woman now. Explaining. The woman looked through her window. Looked right at him. Stared. From the life that she lived, she knew all about him. Mister Myrden.

Where was the fight in him now?

Then the vehicle pulled away.

Randy's apartment was up a narrow flight of steep stairs in an old row house. No handrail. The apartment was behind a door. A small bedroom with another room off the bedroom. That was it. He'd asked what that spare room was for and Randy had said, 'Storage.'

There was another small apartment on the same floor. A shared kitchen between the two units. A bathroom at the end of the hall.

Since he came to live with Randy two days ago, he'd been sleeping on the floor. Randy in the bed the first night. Then on the floor, too. Randy wouldn't sleep in the bed with him sleeping on the floor. So, the bed was left empty. Both of them on the floor. Camping out like when they were kids. No tent. Just lying in the grass all night. Feeling the cool come over them.

'Boy Scouts,' Randy had said. 'I used to be one, remember? Two days I was a Boy Scout. That little prick, Garnet Mercer, threw hot pepper powder in my eyes. Remember Garnet Mercer? What happened to him?'

'Eye doctor,' he had said.

'About right. Eye doctor.' Randy smoking there in the darkness. Lying on the floor. 'That burned like hell. I was blinded. Tears just kept coming for hours. I pretended I lost something. My doggie. Remember? No, you weren't there. Where's my doggie, and the tears. Reaching around 'cause I couldn't see a thing. No one had a clue what I was on about. Funny thing was, they wouldn't let me kill him. When I could see again. Everyone hated the little prick. Why wouldn't they let me beat the crap outta him? Just a little. That's all I was asking.'

'His parents were teachers. Both of them. Remember? His father gave the strap.'

'Christ,' Randy had shuddered. 'Who wants a part of that kind of brotherhood?'

He lay down on the floor now because the sun was starting to fill the room. He thought of going down to get Randy. Out of the lockup. Bail money. He didn't have any. He thought of his lawyer. How much would his lawyer keep doing for him? He was dead tired. He could hear Randy's voice singing a welcome tune as he shut his eyes and dropped off to sleep.

'Telephone,' a voice was shouting. 'Telephone.' There was a fast knocking on the door. Then the word again, like one syllable: 'Telephone.' Silence. More fast knocking. 'Telephone. Telephone.'

He sat up too quickly, looking around, wondering where he was. The small room. Why was he on the floor? He was out. Not back in there.

'What?' he mumbled.

'Telephone.' A hand on the knob. It was locked. He'd locked it when he came in.

He thought the telephone might be for him. It was Jackie calling. Or Caroline. Something had happened. An accident. Something was the matter.

'Yes?' He coughed to clear his throat. It couldn't be Jackie. He stood up, getting his bearings. He was at Randy's. No one knew he was there.

'Telephone,' not so loud now. The word like a hiccup.

He sniffed. Wiped at his nose. Coughed. Smoothed his hair back. Opened the door. A short man stood there. He was chubby, slack-jawed, pale-skinned, his eyes slow-moving, swimming in thick fluid.

'That's not you,' the man said, pointing at him. Almost surprised. Funny. A joke being played. Staring straight at him. Not saying another word. Just staring. Like he couldn't understand the crazy magic behind it.

'What?'

'Telephone for Randy.' The man shuffled to the side to look in. 'Telephone for Randy.' Calling out, 'Randy?'

'He's not here.'

'Telephone.' He pointed up the hallway.

'He's not here, I said.'

'You take a message.' The man grabbed his hand and pulled him from the room. 'Come on.' Off toward the kitchen. The man pointed at the kitchen table. Serious as anything. Like a dog had done its business there. There was a telephone. The receiver on the table. The man kept pointing. An emergency that needed dealing with. That needed cleaning up. He backed away a little bit. 'Telephone.'

He looked at it.

'You,' the man kept on. He shook his head. Steady as a robot. 'You take a message. Right now. Get a pencil.'

He sighed, stayed put. What the fuck was this about?

The man went for the receiver. Grabbed it up. Held it away from his body. He bobbed around. One foot to the other. Like he was busting to use the washroom. The man pushed the receiver closer to him. Stretching the cord. The phone sliding. Almost at the edge of the table. About to go over. 'Randy.'

He took the receiver. Wiped his mouth. Swallowed. 'Hello?'

'Randy?' a woman's voice.

'Randy's not here.'

'Where is he?'

He looked at the man standing close. Almost close enough to step on his toes. The man staring up at his face. Into his face. The man's mouth open.

'I don't know.'

'Who's this?'

He said nothing.

'When will Randy be home?'

'I don't know.'

'Does Gilbert know?'

'Gilbert?'

'He answered the phone.'

He looked at the man. The man nodded, as if to say: That's my name. Get on with it.

'No, Gilbert doesn't know.'

Gilbert nodded and smiled at the sound of his name again. Short, nicotine-stained teeth. 'Who're you?' Gilbert asked. More interested in him now. 'That's Patty.' He pointed to the receiver. Called out: 'Patty. That's you, right?'

'Tell him to call Patty,' said the woman. Dark, lush humour in her voice.

'I will.'

'You're a friend.'

'Yeah.'

'I didn't think Randy had any friends.' She hung up. It was cute. The way she said it.

'I can make tea,' said Gilbert.

He laid the receiver back on its cradle.

'I can make toast. I can tie up my shoes. Where's Randy? He has cigarettes.'

'Randy's gone.'

'Where? Gone where?'

'I don't know.'

'You have cigarettes now.' Gilbert poked him in the chest. Poked him hard. 'What did you do with Randy?'

He couldn't help but feel angry.

Gilbert stopped. He stared at his face. 'You're on television.' He took two steps back. Almost tripped. It was that quick. 'You killed someone. No, they said you didn't. Did you? You're in the colours. I saw you, too. In the colours.' Gilbert pointed back toward Randy's room.

He turned away and faced the cupboard. When he opened it to look in, he heard Gilbert shriek: 'That's Randy's.'

There was food in there. Tins of beans. Stew. A jar of jam. A box of crackers. A loaf of bread.

'That's Randy's food. You can't touch that.' Gilbert

was shaking his head. Kept shaking it and pointing with one hand. Rubbing his other hand in his shirt. Up and down.

'Randy won't mind.' He took down a lunch-size tin of beans. Pulled the top off it.

'That's Randy's food. Randy likes to eat that food.'

He ate the tin of beans cold. With a fork.

Gilbert stared at him with big eyes. He was still shaking his head a little. But it had gone beyond that. His jaw hung open. The offense was beyond monstrous.

When he was done, he threw the empty tin into the garbage pail. Put the fork in the sink.

Gilbert shuffled his whole body around to face the pail. Stood there and stared into the garbage. Baffled. Like he couldn't believe what was left of Randy's food. The outrage and disaster of it being gone. The carnage.

He went into Randy's apartment.

Soon, Gilbert followed after him. 'Who you going to kill here? Missus Hynes?'

'No one.' He picked up his blanket and pillow from the floor. Laid it all on the bed. He didn't have a clue what he was doing. He had a headache. Something close to a hangover, but not quite.

'Where are your cigarettes? In there?' He pointed to

the locked room. Went to it. Tried the knob. 'In there?' He knocked on the door. 'Randy?' He called into the wood. His face against it. He slapped the door with his palm. 'Randy? Randy's in there.' Gilbert turned and grinned at him. 'Randy's in there with cigarettes and colours. Let me see Randy.'

There came a banging on the floor beneath his feet.

'Missus Hynes,' said Gilbert in a hushed voice. He moved his feet away from the sound. One foot away from the other. Like a crack had opened up. Contamination. Or fire had shot up at him. 'Shhh.'

He took the keys from his pocket.

Gilbert snatched them out of his hand. He went through the four keys. Found the right one in a second. He fit it in the lock. Turned it. The door opened. And Gilbert went in. At once, he was poking through an ashtray on a table by the wall. The table was from a bar. He remembered Randy taking it one night. Walking up the street with it held over his head. Calling out: 'Household Movers. Bring out your dead furniture.'

Paintings were hung on the walls. Paintings of people. Of a man who looked like Gilbert. And of a woman. There were paintings of colourful row houses. Of the ocean and shorelines. The colours were unbelievable. They made his eyes feel better. By the small window, there was an easel. A picture from the newspaper clipped to the top. A picture of him. With the words 'The Condemned' written in ink. In Randy's hand at the bottom of the clipping.

He chuckled at that. Watched the half-finished painting of his face. He liked the way the colours were in blobs and wide strokes. He felt that way. He wondered if the painting would ever get done. It was fine just the way it was. The smile slipping from his lips.

Gilbert found a cigarette butt and poked it in his mouth. Lit it. Leaned back to keep from scorching his eyebrows. Blew out the match. 'That me.' He pointed to one of the paintings. Then he pointed to the easel. 'That's you.' He pointed to the wall. 'That Patty.' He pointed to another space. 'Me.' His finger moving through the air. 'Patty.' Sweeping through space. 'Randy's dad.'

He looked where Gilbert was pointing. Toward the far wall where no paintings were hung. In the middle of the blank white wall, there was a small black-and-white photograph. Stuck there with a silver thumb tack. He stepped toward it. A photograph of a young man. Smiling in the front yard of someone's house. He was in a white T-shirt and creased black pants. He had his hands in his pockets. His eyes in the shadows of the sky-high sun.

'That's Randy's dad,' Gilbert said. 'He was a nice man. Randy said.'

He stared at the photograph. He recognized Randy's

dad. But not the smile. It had been a while. Almost thirty years.

'I don't have a dad,' said Gilbert. 'Even when I was small.' He poked his finger at the photograph. Kept his fingertip there. Blocking the face. 'I had to have a dad. You have to have a dad. Penises make babies. What happened to my dad? No one knows. They don't know. Why don't they know what happened to my dad?'

His lawyer told him that it didn't look good for Randy. There were witnesses. Grom and Squid were both in a coma. 'Sleeping like a pair of sweet angels,' Randy had said when he visited him at the lockup. Randy tried to make it sound funny. But his face gave it away. He knew it wasn't funny. Not for him anyway. The comas were a tricky problem.

Willis only had the broken nose. He had walked away from it. Always walked away from everything. Kept on going. Right through anything. Right through anyone. He was one of the key witnesses. He and the bartender. Willis would testify. Willis liked to testify. Against anyone. It always made his life easier.

'They want a statement from you,' the lawyer said.

'They asked you.'

'They know I represent you. They're being careful.'

'Maybe they're scared.'

'Of you?'

'No, the law.'

'A lawsuit?'

He nodded.

'The sooner the better, they said. Maybe—'

'You have a cigarette?'

The lawyer looked at Gilbert, seated in the other chair.

'No, I don't smoke.'

'Ha ha,' said Gilbert. Like that was funny. He even pointed at the lawyer. Laughed again. 'Why are your clothes nice?'

The lawyer smiled a little. 'I don't know.'

'They *have* to be nice.'

'I guess so.' The lawyer looked from Gilbert to him. 'We'll do our best for Randy. Unfortunately, either way, he's looking at prison time.'

'What's your name?'

'Colin.'

'No, first name.'

'That is my first name.'

'Last name.'

'Brocklehurst.'

'Spell it.'

The lawyer carefully spelled it. His hands joined on his desk. His body leaned forward a bit. He was a good guy. He took no offense. He wasn't in a hurry. The lawyer was used to explaining things to people.

Prison time.

He couldn't stand the thought of that. Not for him. It turned his stomach. Put fear in him in a flash. Fear and then dead calm. Because that's where it led. But Randy would ride it out. He'd play cards and tell jokes. Win at everything inside. He'd beat the shit out of the biggest guy in there. He'd laugh while he was doing it. They'd stay away from him. He knew from when they were in there together. Years ago. Randy would be okay in there.

'I can pee alone.'

The lawyer kept watching him.

Gilbert held up his hands. 'Always wash your hands. Don't eat pee.'

He stood up.

Gilbert leaned ahead in his chair. Touched a small statue of a blindfolded lady holding up scales. 'Ha ha,' he said. 'Why is she like that?'

'Come on, Gilbert,' he said.

Gilbert stood. 'Why's she like that? Why?'

'She's supposed to be blind,' said the lawyer.

'There's a thing around her eyes.' He pointed. He looked at the lawyer, then at him. Like they should know this. 'Stupid. See? That's why she's blind.'

The lawyer stood from behind his desk. Buttoned up his suit jacket. The button at the bottom first. Then upward. 'When do you want to give a statement?'

'I don't know. How long have I got?'

'They might come looking after tomorrow.'

'Okay, tomorrow.'

'How about first thing? Nine a.m.?'

He nodded.

'We can leave from here.' The lawyer put out his hand. He shook it.

'Why is she blind?'

The lawyer looked at Gilbert. 'She's supposed to be that way. So things will be fair.'

'Take that thing off her eyes.'

'It won't come off,' the lawyer said. 'She's a symbol of justice.'

'She can see then.' Gilbert picked up the statue. Smacked it against the edge of the desk. The small head cracked off. Fell to the carpet. 'See.' He held up the statue. 'See. Ha ha ha. It came off.'

'I won an award,' Gilbert said. He held up the statue while they walked. Back up over the steady incline of Slattery Hill. Row houses tight to the curb. Takeout restaurants selling fish 'n' chips. People with faces that had been through everything. Back toward the apartment. The lawyer had given the statue to Gilbert. It probably meant something to the lawyer. It was probably given to him by someone special. But the lawyer wanted Gilbert to have it. The lawyer told Gilbert it was his award for being so smart. That was nice, but not nice too. Gilbert didn't need to be told he was smart.

'See,' Gilbert called out. Shaking the headless statue at people on the street. 'I won for being smart.'

He looked at Gilbert. He was thinking about the statement. The details. What were the details? I can't remember. I can't remember a thing. I was drunk. Loaded. Blind. That's all they'll get.

'See.' Gilbert was showing everyone along the way. Most of them knew Gilbert. Knew him from the area. They smiled at him. Nodded. Touched his arm: 'Good for you, Gilbert.'

He liked Gilbert. But he was an embarrassment too. He couldn't help it. All that attention being drawn to them.

A group of boys passed by. One of them tried jumping up and grabbing the statue. Gilbert just held it higher and laughed. 'Ha ha. You're not smart,' he said to the boy, who cursed in reply: 'Fucking retard.'

He took hold of Gilbert's arm to lead him away.

'No.' Gilbert stopped dead in his tracks. His white face burning red in an instant. He stabbed his fingers into his chest. 'Not a fucking retard. I won a prize. You never won a prize.' Then he laughed right away: 'Ha ha.' Not serious anymore. Because he knew better. Looking at that statue. Feeling it in his hands. Like it was made of something he never felt before.

He figured he needed to find another place to stay. He spent too much time in Randy's apartment. And Gilbert was always there, following him everywhere. On his heels. Asking questions. Where are you from? Why are you here? The only clear time was when Gilbert went in a car for some kind of therapy. 'Betterment,' Gilbert called it. What a word. Gilbert could barely say it. Get it out without choking on it. Betterment.

He wasn't one to poke around. But he found himself doing just that one day. Knowing that Randy's stuff would have to be moved. It would all have to be moved unless he stayed there. He wondered who paid for Randy's room. How did Randy pay for it? Maybe it was welfare.

He needed to find a job. That was what he was thinking while he went through Randy's set of drawers. He could stay where he was then. Moving would only mean more trouble. Find a job. He liked Randy's apartment. It was quiet. No one beating on anyone else in the house. Or next door either. No violence in the walls.

The top drawer was filled with papers and junk. Old watches, thumb tacks, nails, batteries, wires, packets of vinegar from takeout restaurants, plastic forks, napkins. There were sheets of paper with the same logo and name printed up top. Eastern Edge Gallery. He picked one up. Saw Randy's name printed there. An amount of money. It was a bill. For Randy's painting supplies maybe. When he looked closer, he saw that a name was printed on the paper in quotation marks. This one read: 'Seated #2.' The amount was for $400. Randy had bought a painting. Where did he get the money to buy a painting? He checked the rest of the bills. They added up to a lot of money over time. On one of them, he noticed that under the title in quotation marks there were these words: 'by Randy Murphy.'

He stood there with the paper in his hand. He could hardly bring himself to understand. He looked toward the storage room. When did this start? He knew nothing about it. And Randy never said a word.

'Hello. Hello.' Gilbert nodding at everyone. 'Hello.'

They all knew Gilbert at the Eastern Edge Gallery. They called him by name. People seemed pleased to see him.

'Where's Randy?' a young woman with short hair and small glasses asked.

Gilbert shrugged.

He recognized the voice. It was the voice on the phone at Randy's apartment. Randy's secret life. He kept away from where Gilbert and the woman were talking. It was a big rectangular room. High ceilings. A wide-open space with an office right at the end. Paintings were hung around on all the walls.

'You have cigarettes?'

The woman said she did and took Gilbert through a door. Maybe it led to another room. A smoking room. Maybe it led outside.

He looked at the paintings. Slashes of reds and blacks that made him feel unsettled. Wounds and curls of hair. Confused when he tried to make sense of them. These were nothing like what he saw in Randy's apartment. He moved on, stepping carefully and watching the paintings on the walls. A lot of the pictures were bad. He could tell that. He could tell they were bad. They looked like teenagers did them.

'Can I help you with something?' The young woman was back. Stepping across the space. Her voice with a shade of echo to it in the big open room.

He turned to see her.

She was wearing a brown turtleneck. Tight black jeans. One of her front teeth was chipped.

He thought of Ruth. The young woman looked nothing

like her. Different hair. Different eyes. But she made him think of Ruth. Not what she seemed. 'No, I'm fine.'

'You're Randy's friend.' The woman had a nervous thing going on in her face. She wasn't sure of herself. Or there was damage. Her mouth was slanted down a bit on one side, but it didn't affect her speech. He thought of a stroke. Was she too young for a stroke? Then he saw the faint impression of a scar.

He watched her face. She looked away. At the wall of paintings. Her fingertips were gently rubbing against each other. One palm flat against the other. Held on an angle.

'Gilbert told me,' she said. She shook her head for some reason. Then she looked back at him. 'Where's Randy?'

'I don't know.'

'Right.' She was a little angry all of a sudden. She folded her arms across her chest.

'Which ones are his?'

'Is he dead?' Her face went haywire when she said that. It filled up with pain. Then she was practically in tears. Leaned a little one way.

He snorted a laugh. 'No, he's not dead.'

'Why are you here then?'

'To see his paintings.'

'They're all sold.'

'You.' It was Gilbert, hurrying across the wide-open space. Shuffling as fast as he could go. Straight at them.

He had a cigarette in his mouth. He was puffing on it and held it between his fingers like he didn't know what he was doing. 'Patty.'

Patty turned and moved to one side. To let Gilbert nearer. She looked at the wooden floor.

'I'm smoking in here.'

Patty looked around. 'That's okay.'

Gilbert puffed on the cigarette. He puffed and puffed and didn't inhale. He just blew smoke everywhere.

He looked at Patty. Patty avoided his eyes. She sniffed. Took a step back. She was nervous. Making him nervous. He didn't know her at all. But she was acting as though he knew everything about her. He wanted to tell her that Randy hadn't said anything. Nothing about her. Not a word. She was entirely new to him. But that might make it even worse.

'Go.' Gilbert shuffled off. 'Goodbye. Goodbye.' He nodded at a couple of workers over by the main door. Young artsy types.

'He'll wait outside,' Patty said. She looked at him with dark eyes. Eyes that wanted in. Inside him. Inside her. Both ways at once. The deeper the better. See what had been done to her. Leave me alone and come nearer. The desperate clutch pushing away. Take me then fuck off. Never and always.

He couldn't figure what she was about. But he thought

she might be dangerous. If not in everyday life then definitely behind locked doors. Definitely in bed. It would all come out then. The harm.

He watched Gilbert go out the front door. A second later, Gilbert stuck his head back in and yelled. He laughed. Probably because of the way the sound traveled. He yelled again. Laughed some more. Then ducked back out.

They owed him a living. Didn't they? Welfare. A settlement. What was the difference? They owed him. Everyone said they owed him. He was owed. Gilbert was on welfare. He left the government office and he was talking to himself. Almost out loud. He'd left Gilbert at the apartment. Got up early to sneak out. If he wasn't quiet, Gilbert would be awake. Calling out. By his side in a flash. Wanting to know where they were going today. What was the plan.

He'd given his statement earlier that morning. Gone with his lawyer to give his statement. His lawyer. His personal bodyguard. Protection. Keep the wrong words from coming out of his mouth. His statement was no statement at all. Said he saw nothing. Not a thing. Blind drunk. He thought it might have been a rhinoceros, he told the officer at one point. Storming through the place. He said it because he knew it might get back to Randy. Randy would like that. Big horn. He walked from the police station to the welfare office. Charming, he thought. Stood in line for an hour. People glancing at him. Afraid to stare. My charming life. What a word: Charming. Betterment.

Uglyproof. If only he were uglyproof.

He didn't want to leave Randy's apartment. There was no job he could do. Concentrate on. He wouldn't go back with his wife. Live in that house. Who owned that house? Some guy he barely knew. Some guy afraid to show up there now. Who was his wife? He still didn't know. He couldn't stand the sight of her. Not with Ruth, either. Live off her. He wouldn't do that. He wouldn't be around Ruth without money. He wouldn't beg money from his lawyer. He would work digging ditches for the city council if he could. Like he used to do. Water and sewer. Healthy work outdoors. The money was good. But when he went looking, they wouldn't have him.

'You used to work here,' the woman at the council desk had said. She was young. 'On the trucks.' She pointed a pen at him. Then tapped it on her desk. Like it was a real treat to see him. 'Yeah,' she said. 'I heard.'

Too old. Too dangerous. Who knew the reason. He didn't recognize anyone in the office. But they all knew him. Knew him all to pieces. Each and every one of them knew about not giving him a job.

Welfare.

People passed around him on the sidewalk. Out for lunch on a sunny downtown day. He ducked into a bar three storefronts up on Water Street. The Capital Lounge. His work was done. His list of appointments: Police. Job-hunting. Welfare.

Nothing wrong with a beer at lunchtime. He was the only one in there. Thirsty as hell. The strange look of the place in daylight. The grey carpet a mess. Too much light to forget. He drank the beer. The bottle was cold. Sweat on the glass. Nothing left to do. Wasn't that good. Just great. A free man. No obligations. He'd have a steady cheque soon. Made out in his name. Delivered to Randy's address. Money coming in. Simple as that. Cash the cheque at the bank. Put the money in his pocket.

He looked back over his shoulder. The sun bright through the window. Out in the street. People passing by. Alive inside their heads. Seeing out. The marvel of it. Wasn't life a fucking joy? The bartender said nothing to him. The bartender read an advertising flyer. Things always on sale for the season. Spread open on a ledge behind the bar. Not interested in him.

He ordered another. Just to see the bartender move. That would be enough. Just to get the bartender up on his feet. A reaction. Move. The second beer was even better than the first. Tastier for some reason. Less like liquid. More like food. Maybe another. No. Any more and he'd be gone for the day. Sucked back into the black filthiness he was feeling. And swallowed. He laid the empty on the bar. Froth still at the bottom. Then he went out into the sun. Into the fresh air. Who cared what he did? What did it matter? He didn't care. His head ached with sunshine. His life. His eyes adjusting to the brilliance. To the washed-out people wandering by. If he didn't care, why would anyone else? Fuck it. Welcome to Uglydom.

He thought of calling Ruth. A sunny day like this. A picnic out by the ocean. On a cliff overlooking the water. His charming life. Lunch in a basket. And then he felt bad again. Always the wrong thing to think. Fucking retard, he said to himself. He felt like killing. Not just hurting, but killing. Hurting would not be enough. The mood he was in. It crept through his veins like poison. Bitten by the sunshine. Thirstier by the second. Randy in a cage. These people walking around. Any one of the people walking by. Any one of them would do. Strangle the life away. He hated them all. Pretending a good life. Because they thought they were it. They thought they mattered. Only their lives. The centre of everything. Every single one of them. Buying into it. An important life. The centre of everything.

The police. The police officers. The welfare office. The woman behind the desk. Why are you here? What can we do for you? Is employment not an option? She wanted the information. She asked the questions. But she couldn't have cared less. What the fuck did they know about anything. A regular pay cheque. With benefits. A retirement plan. A family. Television. Two cars. A snowmobile. Basketball net in the driveway. Kids in day care. A warm house. No one raising their voice. No one raising a hand. Was it perfect? Was it really perfect? He wanted to know.

He stood there for a long time. Holding himself back. Gritting his teeth until he noticed the pressure. Then he gave up. Turned around. Went into the dark bar. Right down to the back. The bartender looked up from the flyer. Didn't even ask him what he wanted. Just nodded. Opened the cooler door. Took down a bottle of Black Horse. Popped off the cap. Laid it on the bar.

No words spoken.

When he got home. There was a police car in front of Randy's apartment. An ambulance too. He stopped where he was. Gilbert. What now? The end of Gilbert. It had to happen. They were friends now so it had to happen. He wouldn't step any closer. Stayed there with the crowd of onlookers from the street. How many times had they watched this? Ten times. Twenty times. Thirty. Over the years. Same thing. Different people. Gone too far. Finally.

It didn't matter how many times. They still wanted to know. To spread the word. It was something to compare themselves to.

A stretcher was being wheeled out. Then bumping down the stairs. Two paramedics. One at either end. A woman lying there with grey hair. Her head to the side. Her eyes shut. An oxygen mask over her mouth. Then Gilbert in the doorway. His hands behind his back. A police officer leading him out. Another police officer behind him. Big men in that doorway. One of them needing to duck to get out. Then coming down over the chipped concrete steps. Like it was supposed to be that way. Meant to be. It had nothing to do with anyone else. One person. Like they were just doing their job. What they had been trained to do. Cops. And their fathers before them.

'Where're you taking Gilbert?' a woman near the police car shouted. She slapped her hand hard against the roof of the cruiser. Out in the street in her housedress. Bent forward. Gone almost wild. 'Where?'

The two officers said nothing. They didn't need to. They were both men.

The paramedics put the stretcher in the back of the ambulance. One of them climbed in there with the old woman. Then the doors were shut. They made a sound that meant business. Shutting. Then the other paramedic hurried to get in the front. The ambulance drove away. Lights on. No sirens yet.

Gilbert was crying. 'Missus Hynes,' he called after the ambulance. He stood still. Like his stillness could stop something. Hold something back. Wouldn't let the police officer move him forward. He shouted out again, 'Missus Hynes,' and the sirens answered him. He was as innocent as anything. Anyone could see that. Anyone in their right mind.

'What happened?' he asked an old man standing beside him. The words just came out of his mouth. He wished he had a flask in his back pocket. To drink. And to share. He knew the old man. Knew his face. But not his name. He'd forgotten the name. Knew the old man's story. The old man's wife and four children. Dead in a fire forty years ago. Pot of hot fat on the stove. Cooking chips. Boiled over. Fat running down the sides of the pot. A stream of liquid flames. Pouring from the top of the stove. Gushing across the floor. The old man passed out on the couch in the living room. The wife and children sleeping upstairs. That's what he remembered about the old man. The old man was rescued. Dead drunk. The only survivor. A burning house. Someone built a new one in its place. And the old man lived there still.

'Who knows,' answered the old man. Without even looking at him. The old man turned away. Never glanced back. He'd seen enough. Went into his house. Shut the door.

The two police officers put Gilbert in the back seat. His crying got worse. 'No,' he said. 'No, no . . .' He shook his head. Blubbering: 'Missus Hynes.' Like she was his mom.

Nothing to do about it. He decided on leaving. Head back downtown. He looked at the open doorway. Randy's apartment. Gilbert was over. Gilbert was done. He would forget about Gilbert. He would shut Gilbert down. He could do that. If he tried. Then tried a little harder.

'Leave Gilbert alone,' the wild woman was screaming now. Shrieking. Gone mad. She shook her head back and forth. Raised a hand to grab or scratch. Fingers bent. Fingernails stuck out. She screamed: 'Leave Gilbert alone.'

That was enough. The action was too much. The noise. It hurt his eyes to watch. He started backing away. It was time.

'Leave him,' screamed the woman. 'He's mine.'

One of the officers held his hands up to her. Tried not to touch her. Plastic gloves protecting him. Wanted her to move back. Back away. But didn't want to lay a hand on her. She was a problem to be dealt with. To be taken away. If necessary. Everyone standing in the crowd. Everyone on the street. Everyone in every house. Taken away. If need be. To keep the peace. The other officer now. With his palms up too.

That was it. Those hands up like that. The palm wall.

He had been turning away. But now he was stepping forward. Direction shifting without him even knowing. His legs. Stepping through the crowd. Stepping past a boy and a girl up on their tiptoes. Trying to see. Moving through the crowd speaking low words to one another. Wondering about it all. Another tragedy. Another man dragged away. Poor old Gilbert. He's not all there. A little touched, he is. Right simple. Stepping faster. Didn't care who he shoved aside. Who he knocked into. He was through the crowd. At the front now. Beside the police car. The officer turned a little. Just barely enough to get out of his way.

He bent down into the back seat and climbed in with Gilbert.

'Slide over,' he said.

Gilbert slid over. His hands cuffed behind him. Smiled through the tears.

'What's your name?' Gilbert said.

He told Gilbert. Then he turned to look at the officer. 'Shut the door.'

'Get out of the vehicle, sir.'

'Shut the door. I'm going with him.'

'I'm warning you to step out of the vehicle, sir.'

He looked at Gilbert. 'How you doing?' he asked.

'Not good.' The smile went from his mouth. He frowned right away. The ends of his mouth dipped down. And tears spilled. Just like that. Down over his pale face. Pouring. 'Not too good.'

'Don't worry,' he said. 'There's nothing to it.'

'This will be your final warning.'

He thought the officer should be speaking through a megaphone. He turned and said: 'It's okay.'

'It's not okay.'

'I'm his father.'

'Ha ha,' said Gilbert. His eyes bloodshot. More tears. Tears like a steady stream. Gilbert fell against him. Kissed him on the cheek. A hot wet smear. Laughter close in his ear. Gilbert's face pressing into his neck.

One officer looked to the other. They muttered a while. One of them believing. The other not. Talking quietly. Like no one should hear. It was their decision. Agreeing for now. Just in case. The door was slammed shut.

Then there was applause outside. Why? He had no idea.

His lawyer was looking after everything.

He suspected there'd be nothing left of his money. He hoped so. Randy. Gilbert. The Save-Everyone-In-Mister-Myrden's-Rotten-Life Fund. He wanted to see his wife's face when the lawyer told her. Not a cent, Missus Myrden. Not a penny. But look at all these free men.

How much would they have to spend to get rid of it all?

His lawyer told him that he might be charged. Failing to obey a police officer. He wondered if that was a law. Not getting out of the police vehicle. Riding with Gilbert. Obstruction of justice. That's what they called it.

'Print that on a T-shirt,' he heard himself saying.

'What?' asked the lawyer.

'Obstruction of justice.'

'You'd wear one?' The lawyer getting the point.

There was word that Randy might not have to serve time. Self-defense.

Change his statement to give them a better picture. It was all coming back to him. It was a miracle. His memory. Who really attacked who? He never thought of that. The lawyer did. The lawyer liked Randy, too. The lawyer knew what needed to be done. It was Grom and Squid who attacked Randy. Willis might tell another story. His word against Willis's. In a court of law. He had no problem with that. Swear on the Bible. People used the book for different reasons. It wasn't just him. Why not make good use of it?

Gilbert was in the Waterford Hospital. The nuthouse, they used to call it. The Mental.

Drinking with people for so long. He knew about the Waterford. People ended up there. Taken away. Committed.

I'll have you committed, people used to shout at other people. Up and down the street. In bars. In houses.

They blamed Gilbert for what happened to Missus Hynes. It wasn't his fault. Missus Hynes on the ground. Someone had broken in. Gilbert there. Gilbert in on it, the police said. An accomplice. They wanted the name of the other person. Or people involved. Gilbert couldn't give it over. He didn't know. Gilbert wouldn't cooperate, the police said. He wouldn't confess. Everything he knew. If he confessed. It would make life easier for everyone. Missus Hynes hit in the head.

The shouting. Screaming. Gilbert went downstairs. This is what he said. That is where they found him. The neighbours called the police. Heard everything through the walls. The police got there in a hurry. They were always close by. Cruising on patrol. Trouble soon to surface in that neighbourhood. Gilbert standing over Missus Hynes. The murder weapon in his hand. He'd picked it up off the floor to look at it. To see what it was. What was covered in red. They didn't believe him. He shouldn't be living on his own. Maybe he didn't have anything to do with it. But he was retarded. That counted for something. That counted the most. What was missing could put you away. Because what was missing made you capable of anything.

Missus Hynes was dead.

They questioned him too. He was a suspect. He wasn't there. Nowhere near the place. The bartender at the Capital Lounge agreed. How could the bartender not remember his face. Still leaning on the bar as other customers came in during the day. Others who saw him there too. Riffraff. He recognized them. Them and him. Together. All those years not changing much. Drinking until suppertime. Until it wasn't enough anymore. Then going home. To see how Gilbert was doing. To talk to Gilbert because Gilbert might be interesting at that point. After a good few beers.

Where would he live now?

He stayed in Randy's apartment until he was told he might have to leave. The place was going up for sale. The sign on the front of the house. That was three days after Missus Hynes's death. Her two sons coming to tell him. Sell the house. Split the money.

He'd have to move Randy's things. After the art receipts. He wouldn't look in the drawers again. He didn't know what he might find. They didn't rent out Gilbert's apartment because the house was up for sale. They wanted it sold fast. They would take anything they could get for it. One of the brothers said that. The brother told him face to face. Like he might have the money to buy it. Like it was a secret between them. A deal could be struck. If things moved fast.

'How much you got?' they asked.

'Let me think about it,' he told them. 'Let me talk to my associates. Give me some time.'

They had nodded together. Thought he was serious. They didn't move Gilbert's things either. What was he supposed to do with it all? He worried about it. He sat on the edge of Randy's bed and thought about what to do. Two apartments full of things that belonged to other people.

He'd already asked Randy what to do.

'Throw it all out,' Randy had said. 'Have a garage sale with a bit of a koolaide stand on the side. You at a little table. One of those little chairs. Knees up to your chin. That'd be cute. Have someone take a picture for me.'

He knew that was not what Randy wanted.

He'd have to go see Gilbert. Ask him what he wanted done with his things. The Waterford. Get out of the house and go for a visit. What were visiting hours? he wondered.

No one living downstairs. No one living upstairs. He was there all alone now. In a house. Everyone gone. Everyone put in their place. Except him.

*

The Waterford was across from Bowering Park. The park was built by a rich family. A long time ago. 'Boring Park,' they used to call it. When they were kids. It had statues from England. A soldier throwing a grenade. A huge moose with its huge antlers raised. Peter Pan with children and animals at his feet. And all sorts of flowers that were never there before. All sorts of planted colours. It had trails through the woods. It had ponds with swans and ducks. People went there to feel good. To throw breadcrumbs into the water. People took their children there. To teach them something. How to be gentle. How to be tame. When he was younger, he'd known a man who stole a swan from there. Took it home and let everyone on the street see it. There in his kitchen. Not knowing what to do. Too big to get away. It could always be cornered. Making that noise. Honking. Its wings spread to seem bigger. The children laughing. Not such a beautiful thing, the man told everyone. Everyone with something in their hands. To give it a poke. Then he killed it. Then he ate it. Tasted like meat, he said. That was all. He was a legend. Swan, they called him. For years after that. Never knew his real name.

The Waterford was a big red-brick building that looked like it was added onto a bunch of different times. It was an old building. He'd been in there before. Brought in in chains. Psychiatric assessment. He had passed with flying colours. Got through it with honours. Perfectly fit to stand trial. Not crazy after all. Like people suspected. A doctor told the court. In so many words. Thanks, he had wanted to say. Now. Invite me over to dinner. Hand me that carving knife.

There was a bus shelter in front of the Waterford. Down by the road. The people who went there rode the bus. Public transport. Public meant for those who couldn't afford anything else. They were the public. As public as you could get.

He passed by the tall black gates. Spikes at top. Like arrows waiting to pierce something. The gates were always open. Never shut. He wondered why they were there at all. Maybe they used to be shut. Back in the old days. When you were allowed to shut gates on crazy people. Keep everyone else out. Do what you wanted. Not people at all. When a person wasn't all there. Anyone could do anything. Anytime. Inside those walls.

Gates made everyone outside feel safer.

He walked across the parking lot. Spaces for certain people's cars. Marked with signs. He made it to what he thought might be the main door. The door he had been taken through years ago. It was locked. A buzzer to push. He decided against that.

He wandered around the building. The brick walls straight up. He looked at the mortar grooves. It reminded

him of school. The playground at recess. There were a
few people out on the grounds. Some of them looked at
him. Some of them didn't care what he did. What
happened anywhere. Where? What? It wasn't their world.
The grass was green and clipped. There were flower beds
here and there. Benches. Paths. Trees. Charming.

Finally. He found the entrance. Went in. There was a
security guard there and a woman in a booth. The security guard was sitting in a chair off to the right. The guard
watched him go up to the woman. A man coming in from
the outside. A member of the public. Maybe he even came
by public transport.

'Yes,' said the woman. Looking up at him.

'I'm here to see Gilbert . . .' He didn't know Gilbert's
last name. He just stood there.

'Gilbert? Last name?'

'No, first. Came in a few days ago.'

That's all she needed. The woman was used to dealing
with broken bits of information. She typed on her
computer. 'Gilbert,' she said. Her eyes checking the
screen. 'Gilbert Maloney?'

He nodded. That was it. Gilbert had said his last name
once. 'Yes.'

The woman checked the screen again. 'Mister
Maloney's not having visitors.'

'No?'

'No.'

'When is he having them?'

'Are you a relative?'

He wouldn't answer that question. He wanted to say: I didn't even know his last name. What do you think?

'A relative?' the woman asked again.

'No,' he said. Not wanting to admit it. Friend. Relative. What was the difference? Better a friend than a relative.

'Mister Maloney's not accepting visitors.'

He stood there. Wanting to ask more questions. Was Mister Maloney not *accepting* visitors? Or was Mister Maloney not *permitted* to have visitors? There was a difference. Whose responsibility? Gilbert's decision? No. But they made it sound that way. For their own sake.

Mister Maloney is too busy to accept visitors. Far too busy. A busy busy man is Mister Maloney. Drooling and wiping his own shit on the walls. He'd seen some of that when he was in there. Twenty days. Psychiatric evaluation. Assessment. Bug dissection.

He looked at the security guard. Looked to see if he had a gun. He didn't. A cartoon. A drawing.

'When can I see him?' he asked the woman.

She stared at him. 'I don't know, sir.'

Sir.

He looked at the security guard. Then back at the woman.

'I have things belonged to him.'

'You can drop Mister Maloney's belongings off here.'

'His furniture?'

The woman watched him. Like the word 'furniture' meant nothing to her. An inconvenience.

'Will he get what I bring?'

'That's up to his doctor.'

He looked at the computer screen. He couldn't see anything on there. It was probably a special screen. Designed by professionals. So people outside couldn't see. The private information this woman had.

He heard a sound. Turned to see the security guard on his feet. The security guard with his thumbs hooked in the front of his pants. That was funny. Bang bang. Draw. Superfast. Wink and smile. Chew gum. Crack gum. Mirror shades.

'Don't make me laugh,' he said to the guard. It was a grumble. He doubted if the words were even loud enough to be made out.

The security guard stared. His face never changed. It was all the same to him. The job. One minute to the next. One day. One week. That was all he ever lived. Inside that head of his. Inside that body. Inside his house. Trouble that he would put an end to.

He checked the door by the guard. That was the way in. It buzzed and someone came out. A man in street clothes. Suit and tie. He had a file in his hand. The door was still open. Enough for him to get through. But it had to be fast.

The man went straight for the main door. Through it and outside. Dashed down over the stairs. Kept going. Into the heat of the sunny day.

The door by the guard clicked shut. Locked automatically.

'Aren't you gonna stop him?'

The security guard didn't get it. Although he took a look that way. To make sure he wasn't missing anything.

'So, I can't see him?' he asked the woman.

'I'm sorry. Not right now. Not today, that is. Maybe another day.'

That was enough. He turned and went outside. He backed away from the main door. Looked up at all the windows. More and more as he backed away. More and more squares of glass. Seven storeys. All the same. People stood in some of the windows. Wire mesh in the glass. Shatterproof. Faces watching the sky. Faces watching the street. Faces watching him.

He thought he heard screaming. Or laughing. What was the difference if you didn't know?

Gilbert. Just like all the others. Nothing could ever change that. The size of that brick building.

*

He went to visit Randy in the prison. Randy had been transferred from the lockup. Awaiting trial. The guard who stood in the room with him and Randy asked questions. The guard asked how he was. How things were going for him. He was a nice guy. That guard. He always was. He wasn't just a guard.

They'd already gone through the box. The woman who checked it didn't say a word. She knew him. Pretended not to know him. She checked the paintbrushes. Bent them until they looked like they might snap. She looked at the ends. Touched them with the tip of her finger. Like testing a blade point. Her eyes went to the man behind her. They shared a secret now. The man at the desk who had been watching her. She held up the paintbrushes. The man nodded. The paintbrushes were put to one side.

'These have to be used under supervision,' she said. 'We'll hold them.' Then she unscrewed the paint tubes. Squeezed out a little paint. She smelled it. He thought she might put her tongue to it. Then she ran the whole box under the X-ray machine.

The box sat on the table between him and Randy.

'What's in the box?' Randy asked. 'Cake with a file?'

'No.'

'Cake with a midget stripper? I got a thing for midgets. Ever tell you that?'

There was a smudge of red paint on one side. Where the woman got a little on her fingers. Wiped it on the box.

Randy saw the paint. His face changing. 'What's in there?' Then Randy said his name like he was twisting it through his teeth.

'Art supplies.' A strange word. Art. He felt strange saying it. Weak. Almost stupid.

'Are you nuts?' Randy leaned forward. Across the table. Whispering: 'You wanna get me killed?'

He chuckled. It seemed funny. Because he remembered. What it was like in there. All of a sudden. He laughed despite himself. His lips went a little numb. Was it supposed to be funny?

'Take it back.' Randy shoved the box with his fist. Like a punch. He was serious. Everything shifted inside the cardboard. Clunked around.

One of his eyes went blind. Like a hand gone over it. He looked at the guard. Only there in one eye. His right. The left one shut down.

'What the fuck were you doing in there?'

'Where?' His left ear didn't work. Like he didn't even have it. Like it was missing. Under water. He put a finger to the earhole. Tried poking it back to life.

'The storage room.'

'What?'

'The storage room.'

'Gilbert,' he said. That was all he could think of. His left arm disappearing. He looked at it. Dropped there by his side. Hanging. His dead fingers. From where he had been poking his ear.

His left leg.

Randy sat straight in his chair. The way he moved made noise.

He looked at the guard. One eye that could still see. The right one.

Then Randy relaxed. He just let it go. Like he didn't care. It spilled off of him. He understood it all. The way it had happened. The discovery. 'How's Gilbert doing?'

He tried to talk normal. 'The Waterford.' To keep things going. But there was serious trouble now. His body.

Randy smiled. Shook his head. He laughed a little. Then his eyes went dark. 'The Waterford.' He laughed again. This time through his nose. A hot laugh. A troubled one. His jaw shifted to one side. His eyes glazed over. He looked away. Banged his fists on the tabletop. A tight-lipped curse. Then he smiled again. Right away. Looked over his shoulder. The guard showing some concern.

Then Randy winked at the guard. Began humming a tune. Put his arm over the back of the chair. Relaxed as anything.

He was sweating. Slick with it. His right leg was gone now. Not just his left one. He pressed his right hand against the tabletop and his right arm gave way. His hand slipping. He almost fell out of his chair.

'Whoa,' said Randy. Standing up and grabbing him.

The guard came over. 'Sit down.'

His right ear.

Randy didn't even look at the guard. 'What's the matter?'

He felt his face go. His right eye. Blind. 'Nothing.' He barely heard the word. A hum in his dark head. A low buzz like an electrical current.

Then he fell over.

Chapter Four

Something was being pulled out of his nose. It was not a quick feeling. It kept sliding out of him. Coming up from his stomach. A woman dressed in baby blue was standing over him. Dragging whatever it was from his innards.

'We're just taking the tubes out,' she said. 'Can you tell me your name?'

He thought for a second. 'Yes.' His throat hurt. It felt stretched. The shape of something that had been in there. Raw.

'Go ahead.'

It took him a few seconds to collect himself. Wondering where he was. He thought of what she asked him. His name. He told her.

'Good. Do you know where you are?'

He thought about that. He seemed to recognize where he was. But it was slow coming. The tubes came clear of his nostrils. He sniffed out. A horrible tickle. Tried raising his hand.

'Here,' said the nurse. She plucked a tissue from the side of the bed. Wiped his nose with it.

'Can you tell me where you are?'

A moment later. An hour. A day. 'Hospital.'

'Good. Do you know why you're here?'

'No.'

'You had a heart attack. We had to operate.'

He heard other men in the room. It was like he was in a stall. Not like a hospital room. The space he was in was narrow. He could hear nurses asking the same questions to other men.

This sleep he was awake in.

'You're doing fine,' said the nurse. 'The tubes have to come out of your stomach soon.'

He tried looking down. Saw two tubes. One bigger. One smaller. Coming out of him. Just something that was there. Not much meaning to it.

'You'll need some morphine.'

Morphine.

He waited to feel a pain in his chest. There was nothing. His eyes turned. Like they were swaying. Saw his arm. His hand. A long bandage running down the full length of his left forearm.

'That's where we took the veins.' The nurse coiled up the tubes she had taken from his nose. 'We'll wait a little while for the tubes in your stomach. Okay?'

He was having trouble collecting himself. Before he had a chance to answer, the nurse was gone. In the hospital that last time. The doctor had told him they couldn't operate. That he would most likely die. No hope. Why didn't he die? If that was what was supposed to happen. He shut his eyes. He was not in pain. Not a bit of it. Not a fleck.

'Hello?'

He opened his eyes.

'Can you tell me your name, please?'

He told her right away. It was expected of him. A different nurse this time.

'Do you know why you're here?'

'Heart attack.'

'Do you know where you are?'

'Hospital.'

'Good,' said the nurse. 'Excellent.'

She moved around to the left side of his bed. She took up a needle and filled it from a tiny bottle. 'I'm going to give you some morphine. We're going to take the tubes out of your stomach now.' The nurse put the needle in the IV tube and let the morphine flow.

It was like he was washed clean. Let loose from whatever was pinning him inside himself. There was nothing to care about. No body. Only thought. And even thought did not matter. Thought was just a softness. One thought, another. They lapsed over each other. It made no difference. It was okay to think. Just to lie there in the nothing that he felt. The no time. And the thoughts without full meaning. Without full weight. It was okay to feel. If that's what he was doing.

The nurse took hold of the tubes. She started pulling. He watched her. She was trying hard. A crumbling edge of sand in his guts. That's how the pain came through. He felt it that way. A crumbling edge pressing away from him. It ruined everything. A crumbling edge of clay turning to rock with teeth. Forming a space. He saw his stomach rise up. A hump of his skin. Like deadness. The tubes not coming out.

He winced. And the sweat poured out of him. Slick all over every inch of his skin. His body mattered again. Too much. The first time like that. His entire body in pain.

'Sometimes we have trouble with these,' said the nurse, letting go. 'Are you in pain?'

He nodded.

'I'll be right back.'

The nurse left and came back with another nurse.

He was still suffering from the first try.

The two nurses took hold of the tubes. They pulled.

His stomach came up. The pain fired through him.

Every inch of his being. Its volume turned up on bust. Pain. Burning bright. Sweat streaming into his eyes. Stinging.

The nurses let go.

Seconds later, he exhaled.

'Get Doctor Power,' one of the nurses said. She looked at him like she was sorry. Like this was the worst part. The other nurse left. 'It'll be okay,' said the nurse. Licking sweat from her upper lip.

The doctor came in. Took one look at the tubes.

'When did he get his last dose?' The doctor knew what to do. No hesitation. The doctor stood there waiting for an answer. This was nothing. Get it done. Move on.

'A few minutes ago.'

'Ten milligrams?'

'Yes.'

'Give him another five.'

The nurse gave him the shot.

The doctor looked toward the doorway. The other nurse hurried back in. Wiping her hands in a paper towel. Tossed it away in the basket.

Two nurses standing there. Ready.

'Just pull it out,' said the doctor. 'Don't be afraid.'

Who was the doctor talking to?

It was hazy and grey. Deeper into the carelessness. He

watched them pulling the tubes. His stomach rising up. Attached to the tubes. He felt it. But it was painless. Just his stomach attached to some tubes. A body without being. A costume. Someone else. Someone who didn't matter. Why didn't they just cut a hole there? Two people pulling at something. Whatever it was.

'Pull,' said the doctor. 'Hard.'

The two nurses yanked.

The tubes came out. His breathing changed. When he inhaled. There was a flutter. Like a ripple of water. He exhaled. Inhaled. The ripple of water expanding.

He shut his eyes to the swell of goodness. His body was okay. His mind, too. There was no difference. For once.

She was sitting there. In a chair by herself. She was looking down into her lap. Frozen. Maybe she was asleep. She had long brown hair. It hung by the sides of her face. But then she moved and a page turned in her lap. A book.

Every breath he took. There was the ripple again. He had to breathe a little at a time. Something had happened to his lungs. Something had changed. He shifted his eyes to the right. A glass wall. A sliding door. He was in a different room. A woman in baby blue walked past. A nurse. She was saying something to someone up ahead. He couldn't hear the words. He heard the sound of a page turning. A ruffle. A flutter. Like what was happening in his lungs. He shifted his eyes back to the chair.

The woman was watching him. It was Ruth. She stood from the chair and came over. She didn't make a sound. Not that he could hear. His ears felt strained.

'How you doing?' she asked, smiling.

Was this his life? he wondered. His head was muddled. Confused. Where did he end off? And this begin. Is this my life? He didn't try to speak.

'You had a heart attack.'

Is this my life?

'You're a lucky man.'

Lucky.

She looked at his chest. 'One of your lungs collapsed when they pulled out the tubes.'

The woman blurred. He heard a raspy sound at his left. Something dabbing at the corners of his eyes. A tissue.

'They cleaned out your heart. Filled a big bucket with the sludge.'

He shut his eyes. Why hadn't he died? Maybe he did. It would make sense. The gentle dabbing at the corners of his eyes. He tried to say her name. Ruth. There was a tube in the side of his neck. He could feel it. His jaw barely moved. His throat bone dry.

'Randy called.'

He tried opening his eyes. Then forgot.

When his eyes opened again. Ruth was gone. The chair was empty. He shifted his eyes toward the glass door. It slid open. A woman in baby blue came in.

'You're awake,' said the nurse.

He didn't know how to answer that. He thought he might be smiling. It hurt. Was he laughing in his sleep? He coughed. He held onto the pain. Like it was a part of his body. Tightened his grip on it. It tightened its grip on him. Smiling? If he was, it must have looked stupid. His face felt that way. Then he shut his eyes and listened.

'Your wife went to get a bite.'

He opened his eyes. The nurse was looking at the screens to his right. 'She said she'd be back soon.'

Wife. Bobby. Skinny little Chris. He felt more pain. Pain broke from his grip. Shot through him. He thought the nurse might have rushed forward. Shoved her hands against his chest and pushed. He was soaked in sweat. Just like that.

'Are you having pain?'

Pain? Was that what it was? He made a sound. His body shifting in the bed.

The nurse went around to the other side of his bed. She picked up a needle. From the ledge by the window. She filled the needle. Then gave it to him.

The pain blurred away. Disintegrated. Smoothed over.

'There she is now,' said the nurse. 'Your better half.'

Ruth came into the room. A paper cup of coffee in her hand. She wasn't wearing a coat. Like she lived there. He shut his eyes. His head sunk back. Deeper into the pillow. He might have been talking. But everything was gone. Everyone. He didn't have to think. He didn't have to feel. He was there. Perfect. One long, silent moan. A gentle hand laid on him.

The nurses were like angels. Sometimes when he'd think of them, he'd start to cry. It would come over him. Alone in his room with the glass wall. Their kindness. Their patience. They made certain he was okay. They checked on him. They washed him. The indecency that they didn't seem to mind.

The doctor told him that every patient on Cardiac ICU had their own nurse. One to each patient. That's how it was.

'You take care of yourself,' the doctor said. Nodding at his chest. 'You'll be like a superman when you get your strength back. Won't take long.'

The doctor told him he had ninety percent blockage in two places. Twenty percent blockage in another place. The doctor told him other things. Dangerously high cholesterol. Overactive thyroid. An ulcer. These complicate healing.

'But these are things we can manage,' the doctor explained. 'With medication.'

He had listened. He had no choice. He wasn't allowed to move his right leg for two days. A wire had been in it. With a tiny camera. Pushed up through him. To look at his heart. He was on his back. His chest a patched scar. When he first laid eyes on it. He felt like a dead man. Cut open. Sewed back together. He was surprised by the lack of pain. It only splintered through him when he coughed or sneezed.

When Ruth was there. The doctor spoke to her too. Like it was information she needed to know. He heard the word 'lucky' mentioned once or twice. The doctor told Ruth how long it would take to mend fully. What could be done after so much time. The steps. The doctor called her Missus Myrden. Who knew the difference?

'Much better circulation,' the doctor had said. A big smile. 'Good for the both of you. A young man again.'

Ruth brought him special things. Kiwis. Mangoes. A full pineapple. Things he'd never eat. He wasn't hungry. He told her to eat them. It was good to watch her eat. He tried not to feel sick at the sight of it.

When Ruth was there. He thought about his wife. He wondered what was the matter with his wife. Why was she the way she was? What had he done to be cursed with her? Why had he ended up with his wife? Pregnant at seventeen. Do the right thing. That was it. It made no sense to him. He'd made a mess of it. Not just his life. He'd find himself moving his head. Slowly back and forth on the pillow.

'They're moving you upstairs tomorrow,' Ruth told him.

'Maybe . . .' he said. He was weak. On drugs. It was hard to talk. 'The Waterford.'

She laughed. 'No.'

'See Gilbert?'

'Gilbert?'

'What?'

'You said Gilbert.'

'Oh.' He tried to think. Slow motion. With bits worn away. Faded. 'Did I say Gilbert?' He watched her face.

'Yes.' She smiled.

Oh, God!

Oh, Christ!

How could she be so beautiful? How was it possible? For her to be there. Looking after him. He didn't deserve her. He wanted to touch her. Have her crawl into bed with him. Her head on his chest. On his bandage. Kissing the top of her head. It was the only way he would believe.

The room upstairs had three other men in it. They all were members of the Zipper Club. That's what he heard from one man's wife when she was visiting. He listened. People talked like no one could hear them. Low voices. But you could hear every word behind the drawn curtain.

The stitches up the chest. The Zipper Club. He was a member too.

'I've asked for a private room,' Ruth said. Sitting in the chair by the side of his bed. 'Maybe tomorrow.'

'Don't worry,' he told her. He didn't want to be a bother. Even if he couldn't stand the talking. The men with their relatives. He was still unwell. The conversations hurt his head. They made him sicker. They made him squirm with pain. The man directly across from the foot of his bed. The man's wife always on the telephone. Talking with her friends. Telling them about her husband. Like her husband wasn't even there. The story of his heart attack. The way he fell down in the supermarket. Wonder he wasn't killed. Cans of fruit falling on top of him. Denting his head. Wonder he wasn't skulled. The ambulance. They were stunned as bats. The whole bunch of them. Like they didn't know what they were doing. Dropped him once. The nurses. They didn't give a damn. You couldn't get a nurse if your life depended on it. Yes, he's fine now. Ate most of his breakfast. Had a good bowel movement just a while ago.

Her voice pure agony.

'Keith Jarrett's coming here,' Ruth said. Lifting a magazine out of a bag.

'Who's that?'

'Pianist. Jazz.'

'Oh.'

'In a month. Interested in going?'

'I don't know.'

'You'll be okay then.'

'Only if I'm alive.'

'You will be.' She smiled. Her hair in a ponytail. Silver hoop earrings. She watched him like she loved him. 'You were already dead. You've done that.'

He stared at her. 'How dead?'

'Completely.' Her voice flat. Too serious. 'Beyond dead. Half buried.'

He chuckled and it hurt enough to stop. He started sweating right away. From the pain. The sweat sprung out of him. He waited. Shut his eyes. Turned his head. Away from the pain. But it wasn't enough.

'I was dead,' he said.

'Yes.'

'How long?'

'A while. Five minutes. They brought you back.'

His head throbbed. It was pulsing. And he was disappearing at the same time. He tried to remember. What had he seen behind his eyes? Where had he gone? He was dead. It had been nothing. He had been nowhere. Nowhere. That scared him. Scared the hell out of him. Gone. And then back. Nothing in between.

'Are you okay?'

He couldn't speak. He had been dead.

'Do you want the nurse?'

'No.' If he stayed still. He came back to himself. More and more.

Still.

If he moved. It was like he was someone else. Him trying to fit with that person. What that person was seeing. He had to stay still. Stay quiet. He couldn't bear sound. Even Ruth. Talking. He couldn't suffer it.

Ruth stayed quiet.

He stared out the window. A view over the city. Toward downtown. The harbour and the hills. Small square houses. Perched on the hill. A tough neighbourhood. The Brow. They called it. He knew people from up there. Two huge oil-storage tanks near the houses.

Ruth sat in the chair. She opened her magazine. Started reading. 'Lunch on the way,' she said. 'You can smell it from here. Yum-yum.'

The woman across the way: Yes, he's walking now. He's up and around. He just went out to the corridor. Now, he's coming back in. He's gonna lie down, I think.

You gonna lie down? Are you? Yes, he's gonna lie down. There he goes. Lying down.

At first. He couldn't move without being helped. He'd try. And he'd be stuck. Weakness. Pain. He'd push to get up on his own. Have to give up on it. It beat him. Let go of the metal rail. Lie there and wait for help. The nurses got him up and around. The slow shuffle down the corridor. It was important to start walking right away. And to pee. They kept asking him if he'd peed. He kept trying to force it. If he didn't pee soon they'd have to put a catheter in. That was something he'd rather avoid. It hurt just calling it to mind.

For some reason. He kept thinking of his wife. He couldn't get her out of his head. His family. He wouldn't go back there. Not to Randy's apartment either. What would happen to everything in the apartments? Gilbert. He should tell Ruth. Ruth would take care of it. You could trust Ruth. He thought of Jackie. Caroline. His life. He kept thinking he should call them. See how they were doing. He didn't want them to know. Not to see him like this. If they came for a visit. He'd lose it. He'd take one look at Caroline and he'd be in tears. They'd have to mop him up from the floor. Everything he could have missed. A little life. He wanted to watch her grow. If only that. That was all. Grow.

I was dead.

He wanted to get things cleared away. When everything was cleared away. He'd see them again. He wanted the money. He couldn't stand to see them in Willis's house.

He called his lawyer from the hospital. He asked the nurse to dial the number. When Ruth wasn't there.

'How are you?' the lawyer asked.

'Fine.'

'I was calling your wife. She didn't know where you were. She sounded a bit worried.'

Worried about what? He said nothing in reply.

'You want news, I guess.'

'Yes.'

'You okay?'

'Yeah.'

'It appears as though we're getting closer to a settlement. It appears very promising. The government indicated its willingness to deal with this quickly. The justice minister announced a special commission to study your case and others. One of the statements he made at the press conference concerned the priority for quick compensation for the wrongfully accused.' The lawyer waited.

'Good.' He swallowed. Took a slow breath. Kept it from going too deep. The ripple of pain was almost gone now. 'How long?'

'I can't say for certain, but it looks like months. It's that close. The government's lawyers called right after the announcement from the justice minister. They want it done. Word like that rarely comes. I've had compensation claims going four, five years. Ten years.'

'Good.' He shut his eyes. That would be good. Caroline's and Jackie's faces in his mind.

I was dead. He wanted to tell the lawyer. The lawyer was almost a friend. The lawyer would understand. Dead.

'They've requested that you appear before the inquiry.'

He thought about that. The words sometimes didn't make sense. Unless they were plain. It must have been the medication.

'What?'

'They've asked you to appear before the commission.'

'I don't know.'

'You can give your side of it.'

'I wouldn't know . . .'

'What?'

He couldn't talk.

'Hello?'

'Yeah.'

'You said, I wouldn't know.'

'What to say.'

'Anyway, think it over. I could be there with you. I'm working to get this sorted out.'

'Thanks.'

'We should get together.'

'Okay.'

The lawyer waited. 'You sure you're okay? You sound a little down.'

'Yes. Fine.' Just that I was dead.

'You taking care of yourself?'

'Yeah. That's good . . . news.'

'Keep in touch. We should get together in the next few days.'

'Golf?'

The lawyer laughed. 'I didn't know you played.'

'Yeah. I used to play.' He smiled at the thought of it. Him and Randy on the public course up on Mount Scio. Having a laugh. Making a mess of everything. Like they were playing street hockey. Rented clubs. Slap shots. The grass so green.

'Okay then. Gotta go. Court in ten minutes.'

'Okay.'

'Take care.' The lawyer hung up.

He didn't know what to do with the receiver. He laid it down on his chest until it started beeping. There was concern in the room. The relatives of the other men. The wife of the man across the way made all sorts of remarks. She really wanted to know what was going on. He could hear her step close to his curtain. There was no greater emergency than her needing to know. If she peeked in, he'd whack her in the head with the receiver. With what little strength he had left. It'd be enough. Knock her to kingdom come.

The telephone beeped for a long while and then it went dead. He shut his eyes. When he opened them again, the receiver was gone. And it was night. Ruth would be there soon.

He was in the newspapers again. On TV. But no one knew where he was. They thought he might have disappeared off the face of the earth. They didn't come outright and say it. They just made the words sound that way. Made him sound guilty all over again. But it didn't work on him. He knew better. He felt like a rich man in hiding. In the woods. Ruth's house. A recluse. He'd grow long hair. A beard. Walk through the woods. Talk to birds. Eat wild mushrooms. Make soup out of things picked. Find a moose and stare it down. He suspected it might have something to do with the pills he was taking. Ruth made sure he took them.

TV reporters talked to his wife. She told them the answer to anything they asked. Anything at all. If she didn't know the answer. She made something up. Just for show. No idea what she was saying.

He watched the TV while Ruth was at work. He

wanted to see what was happening in the world. He never cared before. He watched the news stories from faraway places. These people in these countries. How did they get there? How did people live those lives? How did he get here? In Ruth's bed. In prison. Fourteen years. Owed money now. Soon to be a rich man. Cars blew up on the TV screen. A group of men and boys hacked at burned bodies. This was entertainment to them. Joy and rage. Burned bodies strung up on a bridge. This was all real. For once. He couldn't believe his eyes.

He changed the channel. Two men talking about politics. He listened. Heard the words. Tried figuring some of them out. He got the point of it. Despite the fact that the men were using words they didn't want him to understand. It was a game. A puzzle. People against people. Get them to agree with your point by sounding better. Get them to accept it. Believe in it. People would be improved because of it. It was the solution. If only everyone would understand those exact words.

He changed the channel. The local midday news. Live from the inquiry into the wrongfully convicted. The place was packed. Spilling out into the corridor. *The* place to be.

Ms. Brophy was there. She had a button pinned to her suit jacket. It had 'Myrden' printed on it. Who gave her the right? His fucking name. They interviewed her about her part in it. She said the same things he'd already heard.

They interviewed Mister Dunne and Mister Milton. Two of the wrongfully convicted. There to testify. One was from here. The other was flown in from the mainland. Mister Dunne and Mister Milton. They were happy to be free. That was the bottom line. You put a man away. You let him out. He's happy to be free. That's what he'll say. But everything changes then. It starts with being free. Then what you are after that changes. Freedom isn't the important thing anymore. It becomes a given. Let's see them try to take it from me again. They won't. They wouldn't dare. He could see the changes in the two of them. What they were talking about. What they had learned. What they had been taught. What should be said. Whose cause? Fighting what? Fighting against what? Mouthpieces. Words written down for them. Words repeated.

He shut off the TV.

'You're turning into a TV junkie.'

He looked toward the bedroom doorway. Ruth. With a plastic bag dangling from her hand. Fresh from the outdoors. The air following her in.

'I find it interesting.'

'TV?' She laughed in a nice way. 'I thought they fixed you in there. But I was wrong. They made you sick.' She walked off. In high spirits. The sun was shining outside the window. He would get up and sit outside. Feel the heat from the sky on his face. 'Did you take your pills?'

He looked at them. The bits of different colours. Different shapes. Resting there on the bedside table. 'I'd like to fight in a war.'

Ruth called out: 'A war?' She was putting things away. A cupboard door closed.

'Yeah.'

'Why?'

He stared at the blank TV screen. He didn't really know why. It was just a feeling. Whose war? And which side would he fight on?

'You want to kill people?'

'I want to go away.' He sat up on the side of the bed. Stayed that way for a while. Said quieter. To himself: 'Not a war, the opposite.'

Ruth ducked back into the room. 'Where to?'

He looked at her. He wondered about the man. The man she had left. The man she told him she never really knew. 'Name a place,' he said.

She wanted him to go with her to the graveyard. They pulled in through the big iron gates and parked the car. Next to the caretaker's shed. There was a dripping spigot on the side of the shed. To water the graves. Ruth had

a red rose in her hand. Sunglasses covering her eyes. Her hair loose. She opened the door for him. He held onto the sides of the door. Carefully pulled himself out. The pain wasn't so bad.

'Okay?' Ruth asked. When he was on his feet.

He nodded. Looked around. The gravestones going on for as far as he could see. The sunlight was bright. He squinted a little. Wasn't used to being out in the world. Looked toward the entrance. The big iron gates. Always open. The nose of a hearse pulled in. Shiny black and deathlike. Followed by a string of cars. A few black ones. Gleaming. Then all sorts. It took a while for all the cars to pass. To reach the broken earth toward the back. Where everyone would gather. Where the body would be put. Body in a box. In a hole in the ground. Dirt shoveled over it. No way out. For anyone gathered there.

I was dead.

He and Ruth waited. Then they crossed over. Stepped along the paved path that led toward where Ruth was going.

He knew the way. He saw his parents' gravestones. He passed them by. Wouldn't look. His head gave a little shake on its own. His two sons were buried farther off. Toward the back of the cemetery. Bobby and skinny little Chris. They kept adding to the rows. He had no time for these places. There was no point in coming here. Why here? You could talk to the dead anywhere. Visit anytime. Up in your head. That's where they were buried.

He followed after Ruth. A man wandered by with his hands in his pockets. A little boy trailed after the man. The boy was scuffing his feet. Where was the little boy's mother?

When Ruth arrived at the gate. She opened it. The baby graves were in there. Fenced in. Worn, soiled teddy bears. Little wooden cribs. Plastic flowers. Dolls. Toy debris. Small gravestones. The green mesh fence was waist-high. Put up around all these dead babies. To hide behind. The shame.

Ruth crouched down and laid the rose on the grave. She took off her sunglasses to see clearly.

He stood there. His hands loosely joined in front of him. There was no way of standing normally in this place. These plots all around his feet. So close together. It was impossible not to step on one if you moved at all.

Ruth was saying a prayer. Her head was bowed. One hand on the stone. The baby's last name. The same as Ruth's last name. One date. He looked at the date. That date. It hurt him to know the date. His mind did the math. A shiver rushed through him. Prickled his skin everywhere. Jesus! He took a step back without knowing. Was it a boy or a girl? He checked behind to see what he had stepped on. The space.

Ruth was saying a prayer. One knee on the ground. That date. Or maybe she was talking to her baby. All these years. He wondered what she could be saying. His heart beat faster. His feet on that earth. His eyes didn't want to look at the grave. Not anymore. Was Ruth asking how the baby was? Was she saying: I wish you were in my arms. I wanted you in my arms. If I could only see your face again. Once more. I wish I knew what you would become. I love you so much. Why did you die? Why? I made you. I made you to die. I'm sorry I did that. I'm so sorry. If only I could have been better to you. Saved you. I love you. My baby. My beautiful baby. Her hand still on the cold stone.

He turned away. Went over to the gate. He couldn't bear being in there. The bottoms of his shoes. A child in a different house. A life of possibility. Ruth's house. Piano lessons. Summer vacations. University. There now in a dead place. He opened the gate. Went out. Took a hard breath. Waited. Watched Ruth. Her head bowed. More than before. Talking to her baby. His baby? When she was done. She came out. Wiping at her eyes. After all these years. She shut the gate behind her. But the catch didn't stick.

Chapter Five

The money came through like the lawyer said it would. He was free and clear. Back on his feet again. He had been wronged. The commission had agreed on that. Came to a conclusion. The people who did it to him should be made to pay. Be held accountable was what they said. Who was to blame? No one could decide for certain. But the lawyers wanted to settle it up. His lawyer. Their lawyers. The faster the better. Put it all to bed. An election in the wind. People in power soon to be judged. Clean it all up. Vote.

Ms. Brophy wanted the people who put him in jail to take his place there. The police officers. The judge. She was sure that this must be the way. She got wound up easy. Why not? she said into a camera. Why didn't the police. The justice minister. Why didn't they go to jail for taking fourteen years of a man's life? Exposing him to the trauma and humiliation of being locked away. Do they understand what is done to a man when he's inside? That place. A man who is guilty of nothing. No crime. Other than being in a disadvantaged socio-economic situation. Living in a low-income sector. That was his only crime. The socially disadvantaged in this country will never be treated fairly until people in positions of wealth and power are held accountable for their own abuses. People with status. People with money. They are the ones who belong behind bars. Ms. Brophy said all of this at once.

Then she answered questions.

The money was in the hands of his lawyer. He sat down in the lawyer's office. He was nervous. No reason why. He was almost in tears. It would make him guilty to take the money. Not guilt because of something done against another, but something done against himself. He'd be bought off. All of it worse. His hands were trembling. He joined them in his lap. His wife was there with him. She had to be. The cheque was in her name too. The lawyer thought that might be best. A safe bet. Just in case. Right from the start. Her in on it. No disagreements. Everything documented.

His wife was all dressed up. New coat and boots. Perm. She smoked a cigarette while the lawyer explained. How much was left after his expenses. He took almost half. His wife didn't like that. She smoked her cigarette faster. Her eyes went shifty.

'That's almost half,' she said. Licked at her lips.

'Here is a list of expenses. Court preparation fees. Court appearances. Consultations. Telephone calls.' He handed the list across his desk. Leaned forward a little so his wife could take it. Watched the ash on her cigarette.

His wife looked at the list. Licking her lips and skimming. Came to the charge for telephone calls. Like hitting a brick wall. She said the amount. It was the price of a small house.

'Where'd you call? China.'

'No. Locally. My time.' The lawyer was patient. 'And my associates' time.' His eyes went toward his door. Toward the hallway. Toward the other offices where his associates made phone calls.

He watched his wife. He wondered if he hated her. No. It was something much worse than that. Something not as strong as hate. It might have been hate at one time. But now it was hate worn down. The edge ground off it. Something he couldn't put a name on. So it was worse. He wanted Ruth to be there with him. To see the cheque. How much he was worth.

His wife looked at the telephone. Sitting there on the lawyer's desk. What was that phone made of? Gold. She was making a fuss about nothing. There was no getting around it. No changing it. Look at the man. Look at the office. Look out the window. The top floor of a downtown building. Top floor in a tower. Everything down there. Everything under him. People small walking around. Small cars driving by.

'These all local calls?'

'It's not the long distance. It's my time.' The lawyer tried smiling. He took an ashtray from a drawer. Slid it toward her. It was almost funny to him. His eyes on the cloud of smoke.

His wife looked at the lawyer. She made a face like he smelled rotten. The stink of something she could not begin to trace the source of. Then she looked at the ashtray. Stabbed out her cigarette. The lawyer was quick about it. Putting the ashtray away. He shut the drawer.

'The cheque is made out in both your names.'

What was left was still over a million dollars.

'If you invest this, you'll never have to touch the principal.'

'Whose principal?' his wife asked. 'We got no one in school anymore.'

The lawyer laughed.

He thought he might have to stand up. 'Where's the cheque?' The idea of it hurt his head. Above his eyes. He pushed his fingers into his eyebrows.

'You okay?' the lawyer asked.

He lowered his hand. Nodded. His wife looked at him for a second.

'Don't mind him,' his wife said to the lawyer.

The lawyer waited then opened a neat folder. The folder was white. The cheque was in there. It was on top, attached by a paper clip. Long sheets of papers to be signed. Papers from the government. Papers from the police. Papers from the lawyer. 'These are release forms.'

His wife stared at the forms.

He thought of Gilbert in the Waterford. Gilbert and Randy's house. It still hadn't been sold. Not in that neighbourhood. Things took a while. Things had to get cheaper and cheaper before anyone would buy. The lawyer had explained about real estate. He told the lawyer to buy it so Gilbert and Randy's stuff could stay where it was. The sale was in the works. The lawyer had told him that it didn't matter how much money there was. It wouldn't be enough to get Gilbert out. Randy was a different story. Money bought Randy out of prison because Willis was paid off. Willis changed his story. Willis had no problem with that. Whatever was worth the most to him. Change anything he said. Anything he did. That had worked out fine. But now Randy was in there again. Just after being let off. The lawyer was working on the new charge. It was a full-time job.

'When you sign these, you release the various individuals, organizations and departments from complicity . . . blame. Complete blame. There can be no further actions.

Criminal, civil or otherwise.' The lawyer waited so they would get what he was saying. 'You understand?'

He nodded. His wife looked at him. Saw his nod. Nodded too.

'Who's the money from?' he asked. He coughed to clear his throat.

'The government.'

'You and me.'

'Yes, I guess so.' The lawyer frowned.

'We're all to blame then.'

His wife was still watching his face. There was nothing in the room except money. That's what she saw. Dollar signs on the wallpaper.

'Both of you need to sign.'

He stared at the papers in the folder. The lawyer took them out. He put the cheque to one side. There were a lot of numbers on it. It was hard to be exact. His eyes were shot for small print. His name, he supposed. His wife's name. Printed on the cheque by a machine. There were quite a few papers. Numbers and papers went hand in hand. Long sheets of paper. Thousands of words in small print. They could barely fit them all on the page. What it was they were trying to say. Jammed together like a bunch of people all talking at once. Blurred words he knew he would never understand. There was no point in trying to read them. A code that had to be learned. The law made sure of it. If he wanted it explained. They would be sitting there for ten years. In the end. He still wouldn't get what it was all about.

The lawyer laid out the forms in a row in front of them. He laid down a gold pen.

One in front of him.

One in front of his wife.

His wife snatched up a pen.

He took his. They were heavy in the hand. Well balanced. He thought they might write nicely.

'Do you want to go through the forms?'

'No,' said his wife. She was in a hurry. She had her pen pointed at the papers. Ready to go. 'I've had enough of this misery. It nearly killed me. Waiting this much.' She grinned. Hunched over the desk. Peeked at him.

He could make out the big words at the top of the forms. One word there with all the others: Release.

'We could go over them,' the lawyer said. 'There's no hurry.' The lawyer said this to him. 'You don't need to take the money either. We discussed this, right? You can wait and we can proceed through other means. Handle each suit individually.'

His wife watched the lawyer. She licked her lips. Quick. Then looked at him. 'Don't be foolish,' she said. 'Where?' Her eyes on the papers. Her hand lowering the pen.

Pretending to sign. Making a motion above the paper to sign. To scribble. 'Where? Show me.'

The lawyer waited. They watched each other. 'Your call. It must be difficult.'

He thought of Jackie. Caroline. His sons. His three living sons. The two dead ones. Bobby and skinny little Chris. He wouldn't think of the dead baby. Ruth. If only the money had come earlier. Years ago. The money would keep the living ones from dying. Buy them better lives. Nicer things. Nicer things were like protection. Or the nicer things would kill them faster. It was hard to sort out. How the money would help.

'No. Let's get it done.'

His wife grinned.

'Here,' said the lawyer. He pointed to blank space above a line.

He signed his name. His wife signed her name under his.

'Here.'

He signed his name again. His wife right after him. Leaning close.

'Here.'

He signed his name. Again and again. Mister Myrden. He signed it like that. So there'd be a difference. Mister Myrden. It was a scrawl. But he knew it wasn't his proper name. Mister Myrden.

It took a while to sign everything. Then the lawyer took some time separating the papers. Three piles.

'These copies are yours.' The lawyer put them in the white folder. He put the cheque in there with them. Clipped to the front of the papers. Then he put it all in a white envelope with nothing written on the front. He tapped the edge of the envelope on his desktop. Both hands holding on. 'Done.'

'Good,' he said. But he did not really think it.

'So, now, as your attorney, I have an obligation to mention the possibility of investment. It would be wise to invest.' The lawyer listed off a few names. People who would know what to do. The lawyer wrote the names down. On the back of the envelope. 'They can make sure your money lasts longer. All your life.'

His wife laughed. 'Won't last long. Money's for spending.'

The lawyer said nothing. He'd seen it before. People with free money. Friends and family members with ideas. With plans. Nothing left in a year. Pissed away. The lawyer had told him stories. Before the money came through. The lawyer had wanted him to know.

'Let's get to a bank,' his wife said.

The lawyer stood and put out his hand. The one not holding the envelope. To shake. Then the lawyer put out his other hand. The one holding the envelope.

His wife took the envelope. She made a sound when it was in her hand. A sweet sound. A sound he hadn't heard from her since she was a young woman. A different person.

He shook the lawyer's hand.

His wife shook the lawyer's hand. She liked shaking that hand. He could tell. The lawyer was glad that it was all done. But there was something else. Maybe regret. His name on that cheque. All that time. Bought off. They both knew what they were doing was wrong.

'I'm happy for you,' the lawyer said. And you could tell that he was. He wasn't a prick like everyone said.

'Thanks.'

'Enjoy it,' said the lawyer. The way it sounded. Like it was the end of them.

'What about those funds for Jackie and Caroline?' He knew he shouldn't have said it. Not in front of his wife. It was best to keep it a secret. But his wife wasn't listening. She had opened the envelope and was peeking down. Grinning at the cheque. Like it was a baby. A blessed miracle.

'Come see me.'

This made him feel a little better. It almost made him smile. He noticed that the pen was still in his hand. He'd moved it over to his left hand when he shook on the deal. He didn't realize he was paying so much attention to it.

He kept looking at it. It sat there in his palm. It was shiny. Then he heard the lawyer say: 'You get to keep the pens.'

But he wouldn't. He laid his on the desk. His eyes on it. Like a bang just gone off.

The car that one of the local dealers gave them a year ago was smashed up by one of his sons. One week old. They had it towed to a used parts lot. Scrap. A few hundred dollars for it.

They took a taxi to the bank around the corner from his wife's house. They stood in the normal lineup. He wondered if he should go over to the place where there were seats. What was that place for? When they got to the teller. His wife shoved him aside. How quickly she forgot. How quickly she took advantage. The way he changed was nothing to her. It never changed her. She just got her way more. He let her. He watched her. He would be gone soon.

'We wanna open an account,' she said.

'Do you have an appointment?'

'No,' said his wife. 'But I've got a cheque for a million dollars.' She laughed and slapped his chest with the back of her hand. Like they were in it together.

The teller looked at him. She knew his face. The sight of his face changed the way she saw things. She pointed to the seats he had been looking at.

'If you'd like to have a seat over there,' said the teller. 'Someone will look after you.'

'That's right,' said his wife, smiling. 'Now she knows.'

They went over to the chairs. No one was ahead of them. He wondered why they needed an appointment. Were they supposed to have one? The teller walked off to get a woman. An older woman. Small and fat in a suit. Curly hair and glasses. The woman watched them while the teller told her things. The woman nodded a few times. There was a plan being laid down. The woman came over. She sat behind the low counter. There was a computer next to her. He couldn't see the screen. What was on it. He stood there. His wife sat down right away.

'You'd like to open an account?' The woman said this to his wife. Then looked up at him.

His wife pulled the cheque out of the envelope. She handed it over. Laid it on the desk. Pressed her palm on it. Patted it. Better than words. The woman looked at the cheque. She tried not to look surprised.

He knew that he'd need ID.

His wife took out the papers. 'You need these too?' she asked.

That was it. He grabbed them from her. The woman's eyes went to him. Fast. He took his time putting the papers back in the envelope. Trying to forget the noise they made.

'Excuse me,' said the woman. She went off to talk to someone else. Someone who knew what to do. They needed to keep asking the ones with better information. On and on up the chain.

His wife looked up at him. She was sitting in the chair. He was standing. She smiled at him. She patted his arm. He had done good. It had all been worth it after all. She felt that way. Happy as a pig in its own filth. She rubbed her palms together. He held onto the envelope. Held it against his chest. Against the tender scar that his wife had slapped. Back at the teller. He still felt it. The Zipper Club. He liked the idea of that. Open him up. Have a gawk inside. Close him up. Caroline would think that was interesting. Maybe she'd laugh if he told her the right way. Her laugh. That would be great to hear. Right about now.

'Missus Myrden, the manager is ready to see you,' said the woman in the suit. 'Please, this way. Mister Myrden?'

Staring but not seeing. He came back to himself. Slowly followed after her along the carpet. Past offices. He had never been in there before. The carpet was clean. The walls had pictures of men in suits. Or pictures of the ocean. A fishing boat. A lighthouse. A beach. In gold frames. The manager's office at the end of the hallway. The manager showed himself in the doorway before they got there. He was in good shape. Tall. Not that old. But he didn't have much hair. His head was shiny. Like he had polished it.

'Mister Myrden,' said the manager. 'Very pleased to meet you.' He put out his hand. Shook. The hand was soft. Warm. Like a boy's. A man with little boy's hands. 'And Missus Myrden. Hello.' He shook again. He swept his other hand toward his office. 'Come in, please.'

They followed him in. The office smelled of paper. New carpet. False, hollow walls.

'Please, sit down.'

They sat.

The manager smiled. Like he cared about everything they'd ever done in their entire lives. It took years to learn. A guarantee that his smile was for the well-being of whoever. It got him the big office. 'So, what can we do for you today?'

The options had given him a headache. Brochures with numbers. Interest rates. Locked in. Flexible. They all looked the same. Three-year term. Five-year term. Sounded the same. Except for one small detail in each one. Half a percentage point. What was the real difference? He could make no sense of it. How could it matter that much? What you did with your money.

Pay the bills. Keep breathing.

He just put it in a bank account. Wanting to get rid

of that cheque. His pay cheque. He had worked it out. On the calculator the bank manager had shown him. The bank manager explaining how much interest could be made on the principal. He had taken the calculator from the manager's hand. Done his own calculation. Fourteen years. Fourteen times three hundred and sixty-five. Five thousand, one hundred and ten days. One million divided by five thousand, one hundred and ten. $195.69 a day. Weekdays and weekends. Even holidays. Sick days included.

A simple bank account was enough. Savings. But he could write cheques. There was interest if he left a certain amount in. He could use a bank card in machines. He'd seen people doing that. The main account in both their names. Another account with so much set aside for his wife to spend. When that ran out, she could get more from the main one. Money enough for everyone. They had asked him for ID. Even though the manager said he knew who he was. The manager had nodded. Like he understood. Like he was annoyed at the assholes who had done it to him. Unbelievable. It was. For a few careful seconds. Then his face changed again. Professional. Down to business. So much money a day in interest. They could spend that and not touch the principal. It was enough for him. He looked at his wife. The eyes on her. The face. Drugged out of her mind by it.

They took out some money. A thousand each. The bills counted out by the manager. Ten one-hundreds. Crisp in his pocket. The manager had shown them how to use the bank machine. His wife nodding through it all. 'Uh-huh, uh-huh . . .' He had to come up with a password. It took him some time to think of one. It seemed important. A password. Four letters at least. Numbers like on a telephone. With letters. Hard to see because of his eyes. The manager made suggestions. Some special word. The manager said. Trying to help him along. A word that you wouldn't easily forget. He used 'Caroline.' The only special word he knew.

His wife used another word. It was shorter. She made sure no one saw it. Blocked it with her hands. The manager said there'd be a gift for them. He couldn't tell them what it was right away. He'd have to call head office.

He left the bank and went across the street. Bought two cases of beer. He always liked the feel of that. A case heavy in each hand. Hanging from where he gripped the handle-holes. Anchored on both sides. Enough money for two cases. That was reassuring. They walked back to his wife's house. There was a party going on. Everyone knew they were getting the money. His wife told them all. Faces he'd never seen before. Hands grabbing at him. Touching him. Patting his shoulder. Randy not there because he was inside again. Assault. A taxi driver who wouldn't laugh. That's what he was told by the lawyer. Randy wouldn't say. One way or the other. A taxi driver driving Randy home and wouldn't laugh at any of his jokes. Jokes no one would ever understand anyway. A taxi was what had hit Randy's father. Killed his father. Maybe it was a joke about that. He'd heard something like that out of Randy a few times. Another year or more before Randy'd be let out. Unless the lawyer could buy off the cabbie before the trial. He thought of Randy when he tore open the case. Opened the first cold bottle. He'd buy Randy an artist's studio. With an easel. And some models. Sexy models. Nude ones. That was funny. He almost spit out his beer.

Some time into it, his wife came to him.

'I'm going to the mall.' She held up her crisp hundreds. Eyes everywhere were on her hands. Like it was the Second Coming. He was happy for her. He just didn't know if he cared.

His mind kept filling up with Jackie. She wasn't there. Caroline either. They didn't want any part of this party. They knew better. He didn't either. He never wanted any part of any of it. The stink of a party. The loudness. The drunken laughter. The talk getting more useless by the minute. People should be whispering if anything.

There was a scuffle in the kitchen. Two of his sons.

At each other since the day they were born. No end to the bullshit. He broke it up. They backed away from him when he made the roar. Everything went quiet. All eyes on him. Everything turned on him. In his head. Just like that. He could kill anyone in the room. The fucking money in his pocket. It should matter. It did. It didn't. He pulled the bills from his pocket and threw them at his sons. Other people in the room watching. The hundreds at their feet. It took a while for them to realize. The smiles slowly came. Then they laughed. Like it was a joke. The laughter made it easier to move. A bunch of people went for the money. Like it was a contest.

He stood there as more people came from behind him. Pushed past. He kept staring. Stunned. They brought the bills to him. The hundreds. They tried putting the money back in his pockets. He crumpled it all up. Threw it back down.

Then he went upstairs and got changed. Put on his good pants. His good shirt. The one he wore to church on Easter and Christmas. The clothes he'd left behind. Combed back his hair. Slapped on some aftershave from the drawer. He looked at the bedroom. Nothing in there his. He thought of burning the house to the ground. There was a pack of matches in his pocket. From some bar. He took it out. He struck the head against the strip. The head burst into flames. He looked around the bedroom. How did a house burn to the ground? How fast? If it could only be in an instant. The idea excited him. It cleared his head. He was breathing easily. Smoothly. Drunken laughter beneath his feet. Coming up to meet him. It didn't matter. That was them. He felt fresh. He blew out the match. Dropped it in a glass by the bed. Then he went down the stairs. Not a word to anyone before he walked out the front door.

Caroline wasn't in bed yet. He made sure he got there before the time. Willis, Jackie's husband, wasn't at home. Out spending his I've-suddenly-had-a-memory-change money. It was quiet in the house. Jackie had a book in her hand. Standing in the doorway to see who he was. Wondering why he looked the way he did.

'You're all done up,' she said.

'Special day.'

'How's that?'

'Money came through.'

'Aw.' She stepped aside. Let him in.

'Who's that?' Caroline calling.

He smiled right away. She stuck her head around the corner and ran to him. He bent down. Hugged her. Held on. Picked her up. She was getting heavier. Bigger.

'You smell great,' she said. A fingertip against his cheek. 'You look handsome.'

'We were reading,' Jackie said. She walked past them. He carried Caroline into the living room. He couldn't wait to get them their new house. A big place with a yard. One in the back and one in the front. Green grass cut short. No broken bottles on the street. No busted-up cars with busted-up mufflers. No screeching tires. No shouting and screaming in the walls. Walls without sounds in them. No garbage and rubbish in the back-yard. No scrap wood with nails. No rusty metal. No wreckage.

'You going out to dinner?' Caroline asked.

He put her down on the couch. Sat next to her. 'Why?'

'Because you're dressed up. Are you going to the ballet?'

He laughed. He looked at Jackie. She wasn't sitting. She was standing there in front of them. Then he looked back at Caroline. 'No. You want to go?'

'To the ballet?' She got excited. Sat up straighter. 'Tonight?'

'No. Maybe sometime.'

'They went with school,' Jackie said. 'Last month.'

He looked at his daughter, Jackie. She was dressed nice. She was a beautiful young woman with a hardness to her. But the beauty beat it out. What she had been put through made his skin tighten. Took everything out of him. He felt his mouth frown. She watched him and saw all of that. He could tell that she saw everything in him. He was her father. It wasn't all bad. But it had been. Was.

'Time for bed,' she said. Her eyes on Caroline now. Enough of him.

'Poppy just got here.'

'I know that. It's still time for bed.'

'I just wanted to say hello.' He got up.

Jackie stepped back. He was sorry. He stood there. Then he looked down at Caroline.

'Poppy can read me a story.'

Jackie said nothing. She was searching around for the words. He could tell by her eyes.

'Will you, Poppy?'

It took him by surprise. No one had ever asked that before. He waited for his daughter to speak.

'Sure,' said Jackie. Jackie allowing him to do this. To be close.

'You never read to me before.'

'A first for everything,' he said.

'A first *time* for everything,' Caroline said.

'You're right.'

Jackie didn't know what to think. He could tell. She tilted her head just a bit before she turned away. It was almost like she accepted it. Like things unexpected might actually happen.

Caroline had a bookshelf in her room. He'd never been in there before. Stuffed toys. Games. A little table and chairs. The walls were painted yellow. There were paintings of teddy bears and balloons up close to the ceiling. Going all the way around. What did Willis do for money? He couldn't recall. Jackie worked at the supermarket. Cashier. And she typed things at night. She had a computer. She was always the one who could apply herself. Her and Mac.

He looked at the bookshelf. Caroline was talking. Showing him everything. Pulling at his hand. His pant leg. Talking. Pointing. He thought the bookshelf might fall. His eyes kept going to it. It wasn't made well. It was shaky. He thought it might tip over. Jackie looking through the books. He thought of telling her that it should be secured to the wall. With a small, silver L-brace. Four screws. It might fall on Caroline. It wasn't his place though. To tell other people how to do things.

Jackie gave him something easy. She knew he wasn't good with words. A thin book. She left them alone and Caroline climbed into bed. Patted the space next to her. He lay down on top of the covers. Caroline put a blanket over him. Took her time making sure it was spread perfect. Crawling down to cover his legs. Trying to cover his feet. Then getting back under the covers. It was a lot of effort.

'You're big. I need a bigger blanket for you. Your feet are sticking out.'

'I'm too big.' He saw on the ceiling that there were stars stuck there. Planets. A moon. He felt sleepy. He shut his eyes. He could drop off just like that.

'That's an old book,' Caroline said. She slid it from his hands. Held it in hers.

He came all the way awake. Like a jolt.

'*The Seven Chinese Brothers*. I used to read that a long time ago,' she said. She opened the cover. 'I still like it.' Started reading. One page, then another. Her little voice. So sure of herself. Knowing the words. Anxious to move ahead.

'Your turn.' She put her fingers to the letters. The line where she wanted him to start.

He read two pages. It took him some time. People were trying to kill the Chinese brothers. But the brothers wouldn't die. There was a drawing of one brother holding the sea in his mouth. His head huge. His face puffed up. That struck him. Amazing. Who would think of something like that? He watched Caroline's face while she read more. He couldn't help but kiss her cheek. She liked that. It made her read even better. She was a child. Just a little girl. He could not believe how much he loved her. That it would ever be possible. The cleanness of his feelings. He wondered why he didn't love before. If only it was

Jackie. If only he knew back then. Why couldn't he love back then? It wasn't until he went in. All those years locked up. In a cage.

How had he learned to love in there?

It never worked the way he imagined. He had gone to do a good thing. But it was complicated. He was thinking about it all. About Jackie. Not wanting the house. Right up until closing time. She had refused it. A house from him. Was it her talking? Or Willis. Willis forbidding it. Forbidding a better house. Drinks for everyone. His hundreds were changed into twenties. Every bar he went to. He gave over a hundred. To see what people might think. They never even noticed. It seemed like a common thing. Maybe it was. Up on George Street with the people who were dressed in nice clothes. Why did he hate them so much? Why did he want to hurt them? The pretty faces. They had never been in pain. By the looks of their faces. That made him angry. It wasn't their fault. He kept telling himself. The throb of music that was all the same. One bar to the next. The throb of talk. Of music. Their fucking laughter. Hated their fucking guts. Jaw clamped, he knew it was time to leave.

The hundreds didn't matter. He ended up back with who he knew. With where he belonged. Country music on the jukebox. Hurting songs that almost made you smile with sadness. Because they were about everyone in the room. Everyone was in it together. The door was locked and they could still keep drinking. As long as they were locked in. The time didn't matter. Everyone else locked out. He kept going over and unlocking the door. People stumbled in from the street. The other bars letting out. Shutting down. He bought them all drinks. Anyone. It didn't matter who. The new barmaid kept locking the door. Huffing at him.

'I'll lose my license,' she said.

He gave her a hundred-dollar bill. Scratched his chest through his shirt. The scar itchy.

'That's not real.' She tossed it back at him. Everyone laughed. Looked at his face. And he laughed too. They said his name. His first name and then Myrden. They told his story. They knew it better than him. 'The man in the flesh.' Pointing at him. 'Right there, look.' They knew he really did it. Killed the woman. Everyone knew. But they wouldn't say when the time came. They knew about his money. It was all over the news. What a joke.

He gave the barmaid the hundred-dollar bill again. This time she took it. He kept unlocking the door. Letting people in. It became a game then. The barmaid laughed when she locked the door. Eyeing him. Waiting for him to unlock it. Shooing him away.

'Get,' she'd say. 'Get.'

Everything was okay then. He'd just keep unlocking it. Letting people in. So they could drink. Drink and be with him. To know he was doing good. That made him happy.

There was the house again with all the windows. Under the cover of night. That's how he liked to visit. He was true then. He was real. That's how he felt. The only time. Natural. Dark windows. A still house. Maybe one light left on. In darkness. How he could enter that house. Was able. That had been his intention. But it was getting light now.

He had called so she knew he was coming. But he was late. Stopped at the airport. Ten miles out of town. For the surprise. Pictures of a country he had seen in a window. A travel office downtown. All lit up at night. Couples smiling on a beach. And old white houses. Old buildings. Castles. Colourful celebrations. It said 'Escape' on one of the posters. The surprise for Ruth. He used his bank card for the first time. Had no trouble remembering the password. The taxi waiting. It had taken longer than he thought. Then out to the country. The roads clear. Too early for morning traffic. The sun was coming up when he got there. She had already been awake when he called first. Getting ready for work at the university. Archeology. Or something like that. She dug up bones in faraway places. Went on trips. On boats. On old roads. She had told him about some of the trips. No. Not bones. That's what he had thought first. When they were together all those years ago. But it was about places that were falling apart. Had fallen apart. She studied that. Like bones. Putting the pieces back together. He had laughed at what she did. The explanation. Not in a bad way. Just thinking on it. It was like a hobby to her. That's how he saw it. She didn't need the money. Her father had money. She just needed something to do.

She was in her car when he got there. The taxi backed away. Tires popping over stones. Everything calm in the early morning. Birds making sounds. A few titters from up in the trees. Then the bark of a crow. He stood behind her car. Saw her eyes in the rearview. She wasn't happy. It made him tired to see her that way. It took the shine off everything. The exhaust was collecting low in the chilly air. It came up in front of his face. He stood there. In a cloud. Didn't mind the smell of it. Hands in his pockets.

Ruth sat there waiting.

He went around to her window. Bent down to see her face. She rolled down the window.

'Having fun?' she asked. Her eyes on his chest.

'Not really. Not yet.'

'I've got to go.'

He stood up. Kept his hands in his pockets. He could see her gloved hand click down the transmission stick. The car backed away.

There she goes.

It was a stupid idea. Him and her. Fuck. What was in his mind? She stopped the car. Looked at him through the windshield. He tilted back his head. Watched the sky. Squinted with one eye. What a nice morning. Moving toward spring. The sun was coming up somewhere. It would blind him. When he looked at her again, she was leaning out the window.

'Why don't you go inside and wait,' she said. Her voice sounding different that far away.

He checked toward the house. Maybe it was a solar house. Maybe that's why all the glass was there.

'I'll be home lunchtime.'

He took a look at her. She was straight in her seat again. Her face behind the windshield. She put on sunglasses. Long hair. She was elegant. He stared down at his boots. The car turned around. Straightened. Drove down the lane. The brake lights came on for a second. The car stopped. It stayed that way. Maybe she'd come back. Maybe she'd forgotten something. But no. The car kept going. She had work to do. Her hobby. Nothing to do with him. He couldn't even begin to imagine.

*

He had developed a taste for the black beer in her fridge. It was in tall cans. Strong and bitter. But like a meal. The taste of coffee in it. Good breakfast material. Unfortunately there were only three cans. He'd finished them off by lunchtime. Playing the piano. It was getting easier and easier. Fingers soft on the keys. Remembering. Half note. Quarter note. Eighth note. Running higher. Running lower on the lines. Sheet music in his head. His eyes on the portrait of the woman. The one Ruth thought looked like his mother. His fingers going on their own. Without even thinking. It was almost funny now. His fingers running like water. It didn't look like his mother. Nothing like his mother. His fingers faster. Chasing after something. His mother not even close. He shut his eyes. The eyes of the boy opened. The eyes of the boy stared. They did not blink. What was happening to his mother. What was being done. His fingers raved over the piano keys. It sounded like music to him. Maybe it wasn't. Maybe it was just noise. Music to his ears. The eyes of the boy wide open. It just kept spilling out. Pouring out of him. A river of something like music. Loud. Raving. Raving. Raving. Punch with the fingertips. And then soft. The river of tears behind his face. His fingers barely breathing on the keys. The eyes of the boy open. His fists pounding then his straight fingers. Carefully. Carefully. Touching. He couldn't tell if it was anything. His fingers knew though. Anger, then the lull. His fingers knew all about it. His fingers trembling on the keys. The flutter of eyelids. The boy's. It was confusing him. He opened his eyes. He had to. To make the boy's eyes shut. Two final bangs with all fingers at once. One for each eye. He stopped and stood up. The bench tipping over behind him. Crashing to the floor. The music still booming in his ears. He looked behind him. The bench tipped over. He bent and righted it. Then looked toward the kitchen where she was standing. Still in her coat. Still in her gloves. Her lips parted. Sunglasses covering her eyes. She might have been a statue. She might have been a ghost. She never said anything. She looked like she might be frightened.

'My God,' she finally said. Her voice shaky. 'That was beautiful.'

He bought Jackie the house anyway. Near where she had a friend. The suburbs. He knew enough about her. From his wife. From Caroline. He learned things. Then he remembered. Her best friend, Pam. Pam lived in the east end. Had two kids. Nice house. No husband. Caroline went there sometimes. To play.

He got the real estate agent to pick one out. One street over. A quiet cul-de-sac. No fast cars going through there. The neighbours were busy. Work and then leisure. Kept to themselves. If she didn't want it he'd give it to someone else. There were plenty of people who could do with a house. Plenty of people who needed more space. He could name a hundred of them. Bigger rooms. Brighter kitchens. But those people would turn against it. That house. Live in it and not care. Make it into a slum. Just to prove a point. Nothing worth anything. Nothing ever lasts. He knew it. All that they knew. Ever. Care for nothing. Owed a living.

The real estate agent pointed out the features. He walked around the space. The rooms were clean. The walls were smooth. No water stains. No holes. He looked out the main window. Children playing in the street. Chasing each other. Laughing. He said he wanted it. He'd pay in cash. The real estate agent couldn't believe him. He told the agent the name of the lawyer. He let the lawyer take care of it. The lawyer gave him the deed. It was in his name. To keep it from Willis.

'It's nice to see,' the lawyer said. Sitting behind his desk in his office.

'What?'

'That you can do things for your family. The money's wisely spent that way.'

'Why don't you call Jackie up when she's in her new house?'

The lawyer said nothing to that.

He thought it was because of Willis. The lawyer was afraid of Willis.

'This just came this morning.' The lawyer handed over a small yellow envelope.

Inside was a passport. He slid it out. Looked at the picture he'd had taken. It was a bad picture. Sit here. Look into the camera. He knew better than to smile. The flash went off. Doors clanged shut. They gave him his picture. Two of them. Side by side. And he could leave. He could go anywhere now. Anywhere in the world. Just like that. Who could ever stop him?

Money.

'You can use those tickets now. Have fun.'

He shut the passport. The first day inside came back to him. The fear of the walls. He sniffed. Looked at the window. The passport fell to the floor. His hands in weak fists. His thumbs feeling the cold. The backs of his fingers. Jackie in her house. Out there. In the east end.

He bent for the passport. Looked at the lawyer. 'You went to school with Jackie, right?'

'Yes, I did.'

He just looked at the lawyer. The lawyer had a nice face. Handsome. He took care of himself. He smelled okay too. He could smell the lawyer from where he was sitting. Whatever he was wearing was expensive. He looked at the lawyer's suit. A man who could keep people out. Get them out. Then he looked at the lawyer's desk. At the lawyer's shelves. The books. Rows and rows of books with gold letters. No pictures. No frames.

'You have a wife?'

'I'm gay,' said the lawyer.

You could never tell. 'That leaves you out then,' he said.

'Guess so.'

The tickets were good for any time. Full fare. First class. He had bought them to connect through Toronto. That was west instead of east. Spain was east. Where they were going. But he wanted to stop in Toronto first. West first. East after. There was a good reason for that.

Myrden's Eyewear.

It was no problem for Ruth to get the time off. Her schedule was flexible. This was what she said with a smile. After kissing him. A big kiss. The ticket in her hand. She'd been to Toronto before. She'd been to many places. He'd seen her passport. The stamps on it. The place names all different. She suggested the hotel. They rode in a limousine from the airport. It was long. Plenty of room inside. Black. Shiny. Superstars. The guy up front had on a hat. Just like he thought it should be. Smoothest ride he ever felt. Buildings were lit up in the night. Closer to downtown. He saw the CN Tower. Needle in the sky. The tallest building in the world. Other buildings lit up.

Nothing stopping those lights that made the air seem so clear.

'Is this place good?'

'Which place?' Ruth asked.

'The hotel.'

'Yes.'

'Five stars?'

Ruth smiled. 'No.'

'What's a good five-star hotel?' he said to the driver. Like it was something he asked every day. Only he wouldn't be asking it. If he asked it every day, he'd already know the answer.

The driver spoke without blinking. He listed a few. He called him 'sir.' His voice the same on every word.

'What's the best?'

The driver suggested two.

'Which one is better?'

'It's hard to say, sir.' The driver's eyes in the rearview.

'Which one is more expensive?'

'They're priced pretty much the same, sir.'

'There's got to be one.'

The driver said nothing. Maybe he was thinking. Maybe he was ignoring them.

He thought he might grab the driver. He was being fucked around. One had to be the best. There was always the best. And always the worst.

Ruth said which one was better. She put her hand on his leg. It was meant to mean something.

He looked at her. 'Good,' he said. Then told the driver: 'Take us there.' Like it was a bullet. His words.

They weren't expecting anything like him. He could see that. The man behind the hotel counter. But it was all business as usual. It wasn't enough to smother his mood. Out of the limousine. Clear of that driver. Too young to know anything. What kind of life would he have? In this city? Making money.

A man in a fancy outfit had opened the hotel door. Done up like a guard. But more colourful and with manners.

'A room or a suite?' the man at the counter asked.

'A suite,' he said. Because it came second. More expensive. One step up.

'Baggage?' The man looked at Ruth. He gave her a smile that was different. Like he knew her. Recognized her. It would be easier. Then he started asking her the questions. He kept talking to her. That was fine.

He turned away. Checked out the lobby. Huge space. Chandeliers. Expensive chairs and rugs. Marble floors. Marble statues. Water flowing somewhere. Trickling. High ceilings. Corridors up there. A balcony that went all the way around. You could see some of the rooms.

The doors. Wooden doors. Nicely made. Crafted was the word.

'Sir?'

He turned.

'How would you like to pay?'

'With rocks.'

'Excuse me?'

'That's how I'd like to pay.'

A smile that was tight. Like an asshole.

He took out his wallet. Gave over the bank card. It wasn't gold. Like the others he'd seen. It wasn't silver. It wasn't like any sort of metal. Cards people clicked down on the counter. He'd watched them. Others checking in. What they put down. His card was red. No name on it. Could be anyone's.

'Would you prefer to use a credit card?'

'Use that. Take what you like.'

'Certainly.' A little bow. He remembered the dog. Willis's dog. It had died. Brought to the vet. Hepatitis. It was throwing up all the time. Wouldn't eat. Nothing they could do for it. The vet was a woman. She was sorry for the dog. She really cared for the dog. You could tell. She kept rubbing the dog. Saying sweet things to the dog. Taking her time. He had looked at that woman. That vet. And he wished for another life. Her face made him wish. A woman who cared for a dog. She would care for him.

In a bright white room like that. Her white coat. Other animals everywhere. She had a house full of them. Ones that she'd saved. He knew it. He had Ruth. Ruth was like that. But she stood back. She didn't give herself over. Not all the way. He felt he might love the vet. Just her tenderness. Pure tenderness. Able to give all of herself that way. They had to put the dog down. Kill it. Put it down. They had to kill it because it had been made sick. Chained up outside in the cold. He had rubbed the dog. Watched it. Its eyes. They knew. Those eyes were going to die. Be put down. The dog just watched him. I can't save you. He said that in his head. I can't save you. Tears. He heard another voice: Just a fucking dog. I can't save you. A fucking dog. What are you? Nothing. Dead now. Nothing.

The man swiped the card. 'We'll hold a deposit. Then return it to your account on checkout.'

He looked at the man. It was like there was something wrong with him. His smile. His eyes. His teeth. His hair. What was the matter with him? He was stiff as a board. Creepy behind a perfect face. What did he do for fun? Exercise? Count?

'Here you are, sir.' The man gave him back his card. Then handed him the button box with a cord like a telephone.

He had to move it back to see. He pressed the buttons. Slowly. One at a time. The password.

The man watched down behind the counter. Waited for a machine to tell him something. Then he smiled. Relieved almost. Looked up. He handed over a little pocket folder with two cards in it. He said the room number. He circled it where it was printed on the little folder. And said it again. He pointed to his left with the pen.

'The elevators are to your right. Through the columns.'

He looked that way. Ruth did too.

'Have a wonderful stay.'

'Thank you,' Ruth said.

The man raised his hand like he was hailing a taxi. Tipped up his chin. No need for a word though. Another man swooped in to take their bags. This one was younger. He took their bags. Like they were precious. Held onto them. Didn't want to lose them on the way. Like they might escape.

He liked this guy.

The guy told them a bunch of things on the way up in the elevator. Where everything was. The restaurants. Which food was best where. This was right there in the building. The shopping concourse. Excellent gift ideas. He was anxious to please. He wanted them to know what he knew. He had come from somewhere different. A place nothing like this hotel.

He could tell.

The young guy needed this. He was still talking when they got to their room. Explaining everything. The guy laid the bags inside the door and waited.

He had seen this in movies. He wasn't stupid. He took out a fifty and gave it over.

The fifty made the baggage guy stutter. It worked on him. 'Th . . . thuh . . . thank you, suh . . . sir. If there's an-nuh . . . anything, annnnything I can do puh . . . please call. My nuh-nnnnn . . . name's Jean-Paul.'

'Jean-Paul?'

'Yuh . . . yes.'

'That's okay.' He knew it wasn't his real name. But he gave the guy another fifty just to watch what it did to his face.

The suit she picked out for him made him look younger. Important. She put a hat on his head but he took it off. The sort of hat he'd seen strange older men wear. Wide brim. Thought they were full of charm. Their lives one big adventure. They wore long coats too. Like capes. They went home. Ate something made of grass. Made of dirt. No flavour. But good for them. Sure to make them live another fifty years. Listened to the radio. Fell asleep in their chairs. Going bald by the second. Their reasonable wives wishing they were dead.

'No hat,' he said.

He bought her a dress she liked. She saw it in a window. Black and long. The way she had stopped to look at it made him feel lucky. That he could buy it for her. Standing in the cold. Her face in the glass. Him watching her reflection without her knowing. The window done up. Someone's job to do it like that. It was interesting. Just that window.

He had to insist. She wouldn't go in to try it on. It was too expensive.

'Let me do this,' he said. Her eyes on his face. Because of the way he'd said it.

When she came out of the dressing room. She showed it to him. It fit her nicely. She rubbed her hands down the front of it. Over her belly.

'How is it?'

He shook his head a little. He couldn't believe it. He shook his head some more. Couldn't stop. Like he hadn't slept in a week. How beautiful she was. I don't deserve you.

'It's good?'

The woman at the counter watched him. She knew he was in love with Ruth. He could tell by her face when he looked at her. What the woman had seen. The way he was staring at Ruth. And the woman was happy for him. In his smart suit. His hair combed back. She smiled because she knew the condition. Because she wanted it, too. He smiled at her. This absolute stranger.

They went to dinner. A place they walked by and saw in the window. It looked magical in there. Dark. Candlelight. People talking. A woman took their new coats. The smell of perfume. Jewelry. Men in suits. Grey-tops. Some of them like those with the hats. Women in dresses. Everything brand new. Not a speck of lint could be scraped together. Money everywhere. Hush. The hush of talk. The quiet eating. His heart was beating fast. It was delicate. He thought he might make a mistake. Seated at their table near the window. He'd wanted one at the back. Farther in the darkness. But this was where the woman put them. Where she thought they should be. So he left it alone. Ruth liked watching people. Through the window. Not always. But every now and then. He kept his eyes on Ruth. Did what she did. The white cloth napkin in her lap. The right fork for salad. He ate the salad to please her. The sauce on it tasted okay. But the lettuce was nothing. It stuck in his throat. He had to wash it down to stop from choking.

The tastes were full of all sorts of other tastes. They flashed by as he ate. She ordered wine. The wine was good. Red. It didn't burn when it went down. It made him take another sip and think about it.

They didn't say much. Once he started eating. He realized he was enjoying it too much. His steak was the best he'd ever tasted. It fell apart in his mouth. There were juices he'd never known about. He couldn't say even a word. He kept stopping and tasting the insides of his mouth. The little potatoes in a sauce. What was that? He dabbed at his lips with his cloth. Like the guy over there did. The guy with the watch. He kept glancing at Ruth while she ate. A plate full of mussels. The smell of garlic. She ate carefully. The little bits of flesh. He ate more. She never said anything either. But her eyes in the candlelight.

He felt good about being there. Almost certain. But there was tension building. His muscles going tight. Always during eating. That feeling after a certain point. Lockdown. That's what he figured it was. Eat and then lockdown. Lunch. Lockdown. Supper. Lockdown. That's how it went inside. He checked over his shoulder. Saw someone on the telephone. The guy with the reservation book. Who was he calling? Why was he looking their way? Others in the room too. Looking right at him.

'What's the matter?'

'Nothing.' He said it quietly. Like it was meant to go away. He ate a little more. Forced himself to forget. And the pleasure slowly came back. He tried. For Ruth's sake. He didn't want to ruin it. 'This food,' he finally said. He made a sound. A genuine one. Like he couldn't believe it.

She smiled. 'It's good.'

'Fucking right.' He smiled after he said it. He hadn't meant to be so loud. A few heads turned. It was okay though. It was almost funny. He felt good. Not so bad now. 'Fucking right,' he whispered. Leaned toward her.

'Fucking right,' she said. Smiling too. Sounding like she meant it. That was the best part. The best fucking part.

She was still sleeping. He got up and looked at her. It was dark in the room. The heavy curtain pulled. A married man. A memory of his wife. Of death. Shut down. He remembered Ruth's head resting on his chest. Her fingers moving over the scar. Two of them breathing in the near darkness of last night. He was happy for himself. He slept well with Ruth. But there was something the matter. She wasn't his. She couldn't be. He stared at her. The full length of her under the sheets. Naked. Still nothing between them. Nothing he could do with her. Her touch. It killed him. He shut it off. Then he got dressed and left.

The telephone book gave him the address. He caught a taxi. There were taxis everywhere. This early. The driver was dark-skinned. It wasn't something that bothered him. It was just different. It made him think about where he lived.

He shouted out the address.

The driver just drove. It took a while.

He began wondering if they were going the right way. He watched the buildings. They were out of downtown. He turned to look out the back window. To get his bearings. The tall buildings in a clump. On a divided highway. Everything a little run-down. More and more. Not flashy and made of steel. Concrete. Brick. He thought they might be heading for the airport. It looked that way. The way they had come. He felt panic rise in him. The driver hadn't understood him. What about Ruth?

'Where are we going?' he called out.

The driver said the address. In perfect English. No accent. Like a different man inside the skin.

He watched out the window. Billboards and signs on top of buildings. Names he recognized from back home. Names he knew all his life. This was where it all came from. So many headquarters.

The taxi kept driving.

He watched the meter. The digits climbing.

'How much longer?'

The driver's eyes in the rearview. 'Five minutes.'

'I thought it was in Toronto.'

'It's all Toronto.'

Cars sped by. The taxi driver changed lanes while going faster than he should. The cars all barely missed each other. Inches apart. It was a dangerous game. Rows of cars. Shifting. Changing. Squeezing in. His palms were sweating. He wiped them on his new trousers. His new shirt was white as anything. No stains on it.

The taxi took an off ramp. There were a bunch of buildings. All together. Not tall. An industrial park. New prefab buildings. Lit panel signs. Not on in the daylight.

He felt better when he saw where he was. He paid the taxi. 'That's all right,' he said. Not wanting his change.

He stood in the parking lot.

Myrden's Eyewear. A sign. Mac's company. No one there yet. No cars parked in the spaces. It was too early. The sun just barely up. Clouds masking it.

He turned to watch the taxi drive off. Then he watched the building. It was big. He counted the parking spaces. The ones in front. Twenty-seven. Others around back probably. He had people working for him. Mac had a head on his shoulders. He always did. Did good in school. Despite everything. Despite him. A big building. Wide and long. Going back from the road. He walked to the side. Looked down. Two trucks parked there. Myrden's Eyewear on the sides.

He heard footsteps coming up behind him. Turned to see a security guard. Seven feet away.

'Can I help you?'

He looked at the security guard. The security guard had his hand on his holster. His little friend strapped in there. It was almost good for a laugh. If it wasn't so stupid. He was wearing a badge. A uniform. He had on a hat. Hats were always a problem.

'You're on private property.'

'I know that.'

'Do you have business here?'

He shook his head. The security guard didn't like the looks of him. He could tell. The security guard didn't buy the suit he was wearing. He knew the face. He knew what was in the face. Bang bang. Gunfighter. The bad guy must die.

'I'm going to have to ask you to leave.'

'Leave where?'

'The parking lot.'

He took one step forward. The security guard took one step back. The sun was a little warmer now. It broke free of some clouds. Trying to do away with the chill. His fingers could feel it. The heat. The tips of his fingers throbbing with the cold.

The security guard watched his face as he came nearer. He started to say something. A warning maybe.

Something foolish. Out of a comic book. The security guard hadn't grown up. The bad guy must die. The security guard's eyes came to life with something. He took his radio from its pouch. Raised it to his mouth. His other hand on his gun holster. His little chum. His little buddy. Probably a water squirter.

He took a few steps. Quick. Ahead. He snatched the radio away. Smashed it on the ground.

'Wake up,' he shouted. He did not know why he said that.

The security guard backed away.

He was bigger than the guard. He was bigger than most people. His teeth were clamped together. His jaw hurt. The security guard backed up as he came forward. In his face.

The toot of a car horn broke it up. Gentle. Polite. He stopped and checked over his shoulder. Then he heard a noise the other way. Looked back at the guard on the ground. Tripped over the edge of the parking lot. The concrete edge. The lip. He looked at the car again. It was wine-coloured. Big. It pulled into a space right by the door. A man in a long dark grey coat got out. He was big like him. He pressed a button and all the doors locked. Something beeped.

'Let him be, Tommy,' Mac said. He went to the door. Took out keys. Unlocked it. Went inside.

The security guard was on his feet.

He watched the guard go past him. Then into the building. He had things to ask Mac. That was for certain. He didn't know if he wanted to go in now. Another car pulled up. Parked. A woman got out. She gave him a smile. She walked easily. Was nicely shaped. Not a care in the world. She liked to be watched. The receptionist. Maybe. She was that sort. Pleasant to everyone. She held the door open for him. Said 'Come on' with her eyes. So he went toward it.

'Morning,' she said.

'Morning.'

'The sun's trying to come out.' She watched his face while she went behind the counter. There were three desks there. She took off her coat. Hung it on a tree. 'You here to see Mister Myrden?'

He didn't answer. He looked around.

'You must be his brother or something.'

'Or something.'

'You look alike.'

'It's not his fault.'

She laughed.

'I'll tell him you're here.' She picked up the phone. 'I'm sorry. What's your name?'

He wouldn't tell her. 'He knows I'm here.'

Her on the phone: 'Mister Myrden. There's a

gentleman here to see you.' She listened. She watched him. What was being said. There was a decision. Always a decision to be made. 'Okay,' she said. She hung up. She said: 'You can go right up.' Her eyes went to a door. He moved through it. There was a metal stairway at his right. A factory ahead. Mac's office above. He could watch everything from up there.

He climbed the stairs. It took his breath out of him. Came to a door that was opened. Mac wasn't in that room. It was filled with white boxes. Small and bigger. Filing cabinets. There was another door ahead. Big windows to his left. Nobody down there on the floor yet. Just equipment. Then a movement. One person. The security guard. He waited for his heart to steady from the stairs. Then stepped ahead. Went nearer the other door. He heard papers being moved around. He stepped ahead. Into the doorway. Into the office. Mac was watching him. Eyes there right away. But nothing in them. One way or the other. He was seated behind a big wooden desk. The man in charge. He'd taken off his overcoat. His desk was neat. Everything neatly arranged. Papers piled evenly. Every framed picture and eyeglasses poster on the walls. Perfectly straight. Not a hair out of place on Mac's head.

'What can I do for you?'

Like he was a customer. He sighed. Stood there.

Looked down over the machinery. Through the glass. A wide-open space below. People made things. It was their job. Mac was still watching him. He wanted an answer to his question. It wasn't just conversation. What can I do for you?

'I'm standing here looking at the machinery.' He gave Mac a look. Maybe the wrong one. Maybe the one he used on him too many times.

Mac straightened a little in his seat. He knew the look. It wasn't one he liked. It still did things to him. A grown man. A man all grown up. Almost thirty. Born when he was a teenager. Mac tapped a fingernail on his desk. A beat. His fingernails scrubbed clean.

He remembered pressing one key on the piano. That night with Ruth. It was like that. He watched there and Mac stopped.

'You're doing well,' he said.

'Yes.'

'You deserve it.'

Mac said nothing. This time. He relaxed. Leaned back in his chair. He tapped his finger again. This time on the armrest. Made a movement with his lips. Like he was considering something. His tie was straight. His buttons done up on his suit jacket. He had shaved. Brushed and flossed. Gargled with mouthwash. Trimmed his eyebrows. Nose hairs. Ear hairs.

'What're you doing here?'

He looked at Mac. That question was harder now. Spoken harder. 'Nothing.'

'You can go anywhere now. You've got money. Just show up anywhere. Uninvited. Nowhere's far enough.'

What right? What right did he have? Him, not Mac. He swallowed. Checked the window again.

'You bought a house for Jackie.' It wasn't said in a nice way. It was loaded with bad tastes. Bad smells.

He was feeling like shit. His heart was pressing in on him. His eyes were going to let loose. He shook his head. Looked down at his hands. He was rubbing his fingers without knowing it. For Jackie. And for Caroline. The house. For them.

'Everyone should forgive you now that you've got money?'

It wasn't going the way he hoped. An embrace. Everything's okay. Yes, don't worry. Why should it?

'Well, I earned my money.'

He looked at Mac.

I earned my money.

He hadn't earned his money. He took it anyway. He didn't want to take it. He took it for them. So everyone would be okay. He'd rather have torn the cheque to shreds. Right there in the lawyer's office. It made him

sick to think of it. Bone sick. Fourteen years. Here's your money. This is how we pay. Now, forget it and get lost. You're not poor. Don't use that excuse again. Not anymore. See if it makes a difference. You're free. Maybe we were wrong. Maybe. Maybe not. Who really cares? Here's your money. What you wanted all along. What you were after. We know. Here's our money. Not like us. Never like us. This is how we pay you off. One million dollars. Here's your lottery money. Scum. Now, go fuck yourself.

'You were talking with Jackie,' he said.

'I talk to her all the time.'

He had no idea. He was the outsider here. The man who had made them.

'Forgive the old man.' Mac leaned ahead. Arms on his desk. Hands joined. Back straight. A business meeting. The facts. 'That's what Jackie said. She could almost forgive you. You get old. You get soft. A prick when you're young. All ego. All power. Then it's gone. An old man. Forgive the old man. Forgive and forget.'

He looked out the window. The rows of overhead lights had been switched on. A few people down there. Trying to get started.

'Nobody wants anything from you.'

He turned away. He headed for the door.

'And the worst thing is, you can't give anything

anymore. You have nothing left to give. We have lives. Lives.' The last word shouted.

He made it to the stairs. The security guard at the bottom. Stood there looking up. Hearing what was being said. Watching him. The bad guy must die. That hat still on his head.

He went down the stairs. Past the guard. Didn't lay a hand on him. Didn't even knock the hat off. Out into the reception area. The woman there smiling at him. Her face changing when she saw what was in his face. Not a word to her. Although he should have. It wasn't her fault. He used both hands to shove open the main door. It was on a spring. So it didn't bang back. He was out in the cold. The sun fully out. The air. Facing all of this. Knowing he was hated.

Chapter Six

The fear was something he had not been expecting. Sitting in the airplane. The lights dimmed. People sleeping because it was night. Night was always a problem. Miles out over the ocean. The engines thundering through the air. He could hear them. Thrusting ahead. Into black. The pilots knew. There was just darkness. A car without headlights. You could hit anything. Something no one understood. Black and suddenly there. God. Maybe the pilots knew nothing. He'd heard about some pilots being drunk. Equipment failure. The flight to Toronto had been in daylight. The plane not so big. You could almost believe it could fly. The size of it. In daylight. But there were too many people on this plane. The weight of them. He started adding up their weights. It was dark outside the window. Black. That was it. Black. Above. Below.

Ruth was sleeping. A blue blanket over her. Up to her chin. Only two seats in the row on this side. A wide row in the middle. Then another row of two seats. He was coated in sweat. He shut his eyes. Tried breathing. What he had read about it. The prison doctor had given him the brochure. Deep breathing. When he first felt this way. That fear. The first days inside. At night. Lights out. Trapped with himself. With his head. Eyes looking out into the darkness. Too much of himself. That's how it started. Too much of himself and the airless walls. His mind trying to float out of his skull. The heartbeat. The tightness and choking. Heartbeat. He would kill himself. To make it stop. It would be easier. His stomach so murderously tight. Not like pain at all. Much worse. The breathing wasn't working. He wanted to stand up. It was more than want. He unbuckled his seatbelt. Stood. Almost banged his head on the overhead bin. He stood there. Looking at the people. Some of them sleeping. Some of them talking to children. Everyone trying to be quiet. A movie about something on little screens. A car chase. On land. On earth. Where tires could roll. Where feet could stand. Where you could fall down. A reasonable distance. He was losing his mind. He was sick to his stomach. He was fading. He would throw himself out of the airplane. Into black space. The black would fix him. He would drift. Smack into it. The waiting black. He feared it. Because it was magnetic. It wanted him.

He walked toward the back. Away from whatever.

Just walk. The bathrooms. No one waiting. He stood there. Looked past the bathroom door. Shelves in the false walls. A telephone. Forty thousand feet. Need to make a call. Hello? Yes, we might need a little help up here. Yes, forty thousand feet. No, actually, thirty thousand feet. Hold on a sec, it's fifteen thousand feet . . . He imagined rulers. Inches and feet. How far up. School. A chalkboard. The walls seemed thin. There was a door there. For emergencies. A handle on it. Red letters. Bull in a china shop. He put his hand against the airplane. Trembling itself. Whatever it was made of. He shut his eyes. People believed. An airplane could fly. A bumblebee could not fly. Too much information. It was impossible. His feet on the thin carpet. Steel beneath that. Hollow. Luggage in the big space down there. The shudder. If he jumped it would fall out of space. The airplane. If everyone jumped at once. It would fall into black.

'Sir?'

A buzzing in his ears. A knot in his stomach. His heart hammering everywhere. He tried swallowing. Stuck. He tried again. Stuck in his throat.

'Are you all right?'

He opened his eyes. A woman in a uniform. He tried swallowing. It wouldn't work.

'Are you having a crisis?' She was slim. Looking at

him. Her face pretty. Her eyes all over his face. She could see the sweat. The colour of him. What's the matter? What will I have to do?

He touched his chest. The scar through fabric. He tried to swallow. A thick stutter in his throat. A logjam.

The woman spun to pick up the phone. Her words were spoken the way she knew: 'I need a doctor.'

He turned and looked back over the airplane. Trying to swallow. Like a fit. What were they all doing? The people. It was a nightmare. All of them so high in blackness. Who invented this? What madman? It was insane. These people in a tube of steel. In the black night. Over black water. He shut his eyes. Horses. He was trembling. A horse and carriage. That's how. He couldn't stop his knees. His teeth.

'Sir?' A man's voice.

He turned to see an older man. A man in a white shirt and black pants. The shirt had special symbols on the shoulders. Golden thread on navy blue. Arrows. A pilot maybe. The man took his wrist. Pressed into it.

He barely knew it was going on.

'Are you having chest pains?'

Why was he asking? This man. What did he want? That's just my hand.

He shook his head.

'I'm okay,' he said. Then he could swallow.

'Can you breathe? Take a deep breath. Are you having an allergic reaction?'

He said nothing.

'Are you having pain?'

Heads were turned near him. They watched as though it barely meant anything. Casual but with other thoughts in their heads. Calmness a limited commodity. It might be worse. Get worse. He could set them all off. Double their fears. Ruin their steadiness in a flash. Everyone might pop at once.

He walked away. Past the older man. Down the aisle. Back to his seat. The horror was being left behind. If only he could keep walking. Around and around. Like in the yard inside. The horror in him was shrinking. He sat next to Ruth. Wanting some of her blanket. He took an edge of it. Put it over him.

The man was there. By his side.

'Are you okay now?'

'Yes.'

'Is it anxiety?'

'I don't know.' But that's what it was. The prison doctor had told him about it. Given over a pamphlet. He had read about it. Everything he felt listed there. He had left the pamphlet in the doctor's office. Not something he wanted in his cell. Not something others should see. He thought he was through with all that. But it came back. Sometimes at night. 'Yes,' he admitted.

'Do you want something for it?'

He wouldn't look at the man. 'No, I'm fine.' Stared straight ahead. The back of the seat in front of him. The tray that came down. He shut his eyes. He might punch out a window. Punch a hole in the wall. Help his lungs to more air.

The man said nothing for a while. Then: 'If you need anything, just notify one of the flight attendants. This button here.'

He pretended he was asleep. The trembling was dying down. The God-awful bone-chill. He was almost warm again. Ruth's body next to him. He wanted to curl into her.

The man was still there. He hadn't moved.

He had his eyes closed but he knew the man was still there. Watching. Waiting. The presence of a body. Next to him. He never moved a muscle. Expected a flashlight aimed at him. Bright light on his face to be certain. The shiver came only in spurts. He settled down. And the man was satisfied. The man went away.

The air was different. It hit him when he stepped off. Into the sun. The heat was blazing. Dead hot. Dry. Toward the building there were guards. They had machine guns.

Dogs. This was a vacation. Scare the hell out of you. First thing.

Ruth looked up at the sky. Everything brilliant. They walked in a line to the building. Stepped inside. He thought they should stamp his passport. He had it in his shirt pocket. Always there. He knew where it was. Proud of it. But they didn't. They just looked at it. His picture. Him. He wanted that mark. That stamp. To show where he'd been. How far away he could go.

People were speaking another language. How great was that. Who would ever understand him here? It was good. It made him feel better. In hiding. No one knew a thing about him. All strangers. No one stopping him on the street.

The bags took a while to get to them. Finally they came. Not lost at all. Almost the last ones.

The taxi driver was small and demented. That's what Ruth called him after. Demented. He grabbed their bags. Wouldn't let them touch a single suitcase. Kept pointing to the taxi. Tipping his head. He wanted them in the car. The driver lifted the big suitcases all by himself. A wiry man. Lots of energy. Bad news. He tossed the suitcases into the trunk. Not a problem. Wiped his palms together with that wild smile. Slammed the trunk. He smiled again. Wilder. He laughed all the time. Did about three hundred. Kept checking the rearview. Like it was a circus ride.

Faster? His eyebrows raised. Fun? The speed alone was enough to put him back in the place. Unsteady. Pure nerves.

Ruth held his hand. Tighter and then looser. Like breathing. The way it was held. Around corners.

He didn't want to say anything. Pinned one way. Pinned the other. Then he had to: 'Slow down.'

'*Qué?*'

'Slow down.'

The taxi driver laughed. Eyes in the rearview. Eyebrows raised. Welcome to my country. Almost missed a bend in the road. The ocean down there. Way far down deep. Fuck.

Ruth squeezed his hand tighter. 'Isn't this lovely,' she said. Her teeth clamped tight.

They did not crash. They did not die. This was enough to celebrate. Forget the idea of a vacation. They were alive. Out of the taxi. They almost cheered. Grabbed at each other. They were touching that way. Nervous happy. Survivors. He wouldn't let the driver near their bags. He took them. Like no weight could ever be too heavy. Everything light as a feather after that.

Ruth paid the driver whatever. Anything. 'Maybe they do that on purpose.' On their way to the hotel entrance. Putting her wallet in her purse.

'What?' he asked.

'Almost kill you, so you feel happy just to be here. Alive. Maybe it's in their tourist handbook.'

He smiled at her. He could see the ocean off to his left. People strolling on a wide walkway beside it. He carried the bags in through the sliding door. The hotel was the sort of place he liked. Reasonable furniture. The rugs well used. People had come and gone. Plenty of people. From all over the world.

The young man at the desk was busy. In a dark green uniform. He wasn't friendly. Not even trying. Efficient. This was enough. Couldn't care less about them. He was busy. But he wasn't rude. He spoke quickly. Made motions with his hands for them to come nearer. '*Sí*,' he said. When he was done with them he clapped his hands together. Almost smiled. Nodded. 'Enjoy.' That was it. He wasn't giving any more. His eyes on the next person.

The hotel was made of brown brick. A big complex. The hotel door was opened with a real key. He liked that. A key on a piece of orange plastic. One you fit in a lock. No flashing lights like in Toronto. No electronic click. The room had two small beds. A balcony. A telephone that looked thirty years old. No buttons on it. No dialer. No television. He went out on the balcony. There was a pink tennis court down below. The ocean to his left. Small boats. Big grassy umbrellas. The colour of old straw. Long wooden chairs. Where people might take in the sun. But it was too late in the day to be stretched out there. More buildings along the beach. Then white houses. Small white houses that all looked the same. Red tiles on their roofs. Close together. He wanted to get lost in that. Narrow streets you could barely see.

Ruth came up behind him. The sun was going down. Everything was a little orange. Warm. Pleasant. Quiet. He liked it. How it brought out nothing in his head.

'Is this okay?' he asked.

'What do you think?'

'You know me.' Still facing the window.

'Yeah.' She was talking differently. Softer. She walked slower. Moved slower. Maybe it was this place. The way he saw her when he turned. The light. Maybe she was just tired. Maybe a country could change her. Just like that. Being in a place that wasn't her place.

'Anything's okay with me.' He couldn't keep his eyes off the view.

'Well, this is fine then.' She touched his shoulder. She gently kissed him on the cheek. Close to his ear.

He knew it was more than that. What she meant. He understood. Because he felt that kiss open a clearing.

It was warm enough at ten o'clock at night. He could walk around in a shirt. The air was easy to breathe. Fresh.

Not hot anymore. Not a speck of humidity. They walked down streets that had white houses on both sides. All connected. Like row houses, only prettier. Fancy wooden doors. All colours. Signs out over some. A restaurant. A bar. The wooden shutters opened behind steel bars. Why the bars? Because of the crime? Not in this pretty place. He could see in. People sitting on stools. Drinking. Having a good time. Voices and laughter carrying. No one caring who heard.

It was hard to believe where he was. Every now and then he felt the fullness of it. Rising up in him. The different sights in this town he did not know. How easy it was to get here. Only so many hours. His feet on the ground again. The place he had left behind him. No one could touch him here.

Around the corner the street got wider. There were tables and chairs outside. Canopies stretching from restaurant fronts. People eating. Children eating with their families. Every time he saw a child. The smallness. He felt something was wrong with him.

'Where do you want to eat?' Ruth was walking by his side. Interested in everything. Her eyes taking in the details.

He shrugged.

'Stupid question.'

'I don't know here.'

'Me neither. Let's just pick a place.'

He liked that she had never been here before. 'Some-place with food.'

'They probably all have food.' She looked at his face. 'You're hungry.'

'Yeah.'

'Easy to tell.'

'Am I horrible?'

'No more than usual.' She took his arm. 'You just have an edge tonight.'

They picked a place with white-and-blue tablecloths and sat outside. There was a couple across from them. The man with white hair and a bright pink face. Puffy cheeks. White shorts. An orange shirt with short sleeves. He kept glancing over. Eating. Chewing. Waiting for some-thing to happen.

He heard the man was speaking English. With an accent. The man did all the talking. Wouldn't keep quiet about everything he saw. Everything he thought. The woman listened. She was quiet. Nice-looking. Her eyes on her bowl. Hidden. Slowly drinking her soup. Manners to burn.

Ruth ordered and the waiter took the menu. He did it fast. Glanced around at the other tables. Making sure.

'Thank you,' she said.

The waiter moved away.

The man with the pink face leaned toward them in his chair.

'You're American.'

Ruth said: 'No, Canadian.'

He ignored the man and woman. Didn't know what they wanted.

Ruth put her foot against his leg. Under the table. It meant for him to pay attention. Maybe. Or meant for him to get her out of it. Which was it? He looked at her face. Nothing obvious there. Then he watched the man. The man was eating. And talking. Chewing and watching. In a hurry to figure them out. To get said what needed to be said. While he chewed.

'You've just arrived,' said the man. 'I could tell by the absence of pigment.' He pointed at them with his fork. At Ruth. Then at him. 'The tan. You haven't any to speak of.'

He nodded. Smiled a little. The man was interesting. A bit of a fool. The wife was still drinking soup. Hunched a little forward. Not a sound. Spoon up. Spoon down. Smooth. Like they might take the bowl away. Like someone might realize.

'Where have you come from?'

He thought of saying something. But stopped himself. It probably wouldn't be funny.

Ruth told the man.

'Ah, yes, Canada. Right.' The man said the name in a strange way. Can-Na-Da. 'We're from England.' He said

-248-

it like they wouldn't understand. Would never understand. Could never grasp what it meant. Like he was going to spell it out for them. 'Lancashire. I'm in textiles.' The man's eyes went from Ruth to him. Back to Ruth. The man was expecting. To hear what they did. Or what they thought of what he did.

He thought of saying, I'm in murder. Fresh out of confinement. Looking for new prospects. He watched the tablecloth. Straightened a spoon. A basket of bread was set down. Two glasses of red wine.

The man went back to his eating. Used his fork and knife in an interesting way. The fork backwards. Clearing food from his teeth with his tongue. Pushing food around on his plate. Then in his cheeks. Eyes watching them. Every now and then. Putting it all together. As best he could.

'Hmmm,' said the man. But more to himself. While he chewed.

The man's wife. Not a word. Not yet.

He ate the bread. He drank the wine. They were good together. Bread and wine.

'We must have drinks later.' The man's voice. Through the food. 'Where are you staying?' He coughed quickly to clear his throat. Might have been the start of choking. Unfortunately. It didn't last long. The man wiped at his mouth. Something pushed into the napkin with his tongue. Folded over. Hidden away. Laid down.

'Las Palmeras.'

He was surprised at how she said it. That she told the man. But also how she sounded. Like the words were natural to her. Had existed inside her forever. Maybe she spoke Spanish. He never asked.

'Right.' The man raised his wineglass. His wife watched them through the corners of her eyes. Good looks made more attractive by her dark stare. She ate her soup. Up and down. Up and down. Not a sound. Her eyes on him more than Ruth. Something there that she was keeping. To herself.

The man from England was named Lawrence. Larry. Larry. No, call me Larry for God's sake. Christ! He blew air up at his nose. Lawrence. He tutted and shook his head. He was loaded. He was a writer, he said. The textile business was his father's. Not his true calling. Was fashioned for other things. Although he took the money from it. He laughed at that. My labour of love. Writing. Wrote travel books. About places no one wanted to go. But this place. This place was a holiday for him. He made a man out of his two fingers when he told them that. He walked the little man around on the bar. Back and forth then in circles.

'Travel,' said Larry. 'Little little.'

His wife had become full of herself. Grand. Pushed

back her hair. Or fluffed it. Bracelets on her arms. Jangling. The only thing making a sound on her. She drank brandy and sat at the end of the bar. Her head back a little. Her long sleek black hair. She watched them and sipped her drink. She watched everything. Took it all in. Deciding on when it would be right for her. Every now and then something caught her eye and she stared. To get every last thing out of it. Then she faced him again. Her head back a bit. In dark colours. A long skirt. A dark blouse with dark beads at her throat. The soup was all she had eaten.

Ruth was having a good time. Talking to Larry. Telling stories of travels. They were all a little drunk. The woman behind the bar was young and blonde. Real blonde hair. All different shades. Made that way from sunlight. The hair he always thought of. When thinking of love. She was from Australia she said. She sounded it. He liked her face. The friendliness that she had in her. The big smile. Hands in her front jean pockets. When she wasn't busy. Swiveling her hips. Liked her more and more. It was a surprise. So many people from England. From Ireland. From Australia. In Spain. Pubs everywhere.

'The booze is so bloody cheap here,' Larry said. Like it was an insane secret. He looked around to see if anyone had heard. He leaned closer. Lowered his voice. 'It's fucking brilliant.'

He sipped his beer. It wasn't bad. San Miguel. He thought of peeling off the label to take home with him. To show Randy. He'd bring Randy home a case of it. San Miguel. If he was allowed to. Randy would like that. And something Spanish. A little flamenco dancer. A statue doll with a lacy dress. Show Randy the pictures that Ruth would take. And Caroline. Jackie too. Gifts for them. Plastic bulls and castanets for Caroline's new room. Maybe a little purse. Plenty of purses around. Leather shops. Jackie would love a vacation. That was what he would do for her next. He had picked Jackie and Caroline up in a taxi. Tricked them. Told them he wanted to buy Caroline an outfit at the mall. A few gifts for being so good. It was an effort. Just to get Jackie to agree. But the taxi went in the other direction. Away from the mall. Toward the east end. Where's this? Jackie had asked. When the taxi stopped. She almost wouldn't get out. Like it was a trap. Caroline got out. He bent to her. He whispered in her ear: It's yours. She looked at the house because he was looking there. At the front door. She screamed. Jumped up and down. The house. Yes. The house. Caroline raced up the stairs. Two steps at a time. Two flights of concrete outside. Grabbing at the railing. They went inside. Caroline first. He gave her the shiny key to open the door. The new pink one he had cut just for her. She couldn't believe it. The goodness beaming out of her.

Jackie still on the steps. One slow step at a time. Watching the opened door. The taxi driving off. Caroline inside the new house. He thought he might burst with joy. Caroline running up the hallway. Stopping in a doorway. Her face. Her bedroom. Not knowing it. Her jaw hung open. Looking at him. Look at all this stuff. Look. She went in. It's yours. Mine? Yes. Yours. All of it. She grabbed hold of him. Held on. Kept holding on. Hugging. Squeezing. She started crying. Not like she was happy. But she was sick. Sobbing a bit. So that Jackie came. What's the matter? All of this is mine. She was happy then. After all. He couldn't tell. Then he could. She went around touching the stuffed toys. Not holding them yet. Not knowing if it was okay. Someone else's. The stacks of games in their boxes. The plastic still on. The toys in their boxes. The posters on the walls. Horses. Puppies. Kittens. Jackie looking at him like she didn't know. Who he was. Leaving the room. Quickly. She was mad with him. The sound she made. Leaving. She wasn't in the kitchen. Like he expected. Looked in there. Another mistake. Electric appliances on the counter. Still in their boxes. Food processor. Hand mixer. Electric kettle. Toaster. Four slices. Big slots. Daddy, she said. The way she said it was enough to cripple him. Like she was hurt. Someone had hurt her. Mistake after mistake. He went to where she was. In the living room. Staring at the art. Paintings he bought at different galleries. Downtown. Paintings he had picked out for her. Ones he thought she would like. Ones he felt she would like. Jackie looking at them. Turning to face him. Wiping a tear from her cheek with her palm. Oh, Daddy. She wasn't mad at him at all. Jackie. His little girl.

They had moved in. Jackie and Caroline. They had agreed. To live in the house he had bought for them.

'Who do you think you are?'

He came out of it. That sweet feeling from remembering. He looked over at Larry's wife. She was watching him. He wondered if she'd said that. It was like she'd said nothing. Maybe it was just in his head. His own voice.

'Yes, you,' said Larry's wife. Her voice deep. Almost a growl.

Larry looked over at her right away. He said something low. Under his breath. Like a curse. Ruth looked over too. A few other people at tables by the door. It was a small place. A flash had gone off. Moments ago. Ruth taking a picture. He realized now. While he was remembering.

He took a sip of his beer. Laid down the empty bottle. Picked up the other one. The one Larry had bought. He kept buying. He wouldn't let anyone else buy. Larry with all his textile money. Traveling with it. Stuffed in his wallet. He took it out. Left it open while he asked the price. So people would know.

Larry's wife sipped her drink. Holding the glass with both hands. Brown eyes. Thick black eyeliner. She never said anything else. She just stared at him. Everyone left her alone. She was marked now though. Had to be watched.

The place lost its mood after that. They all thought of leaving. Felt it was necessary. Larry was up ahead. The tour guy. The travel writer. He knew everything. Nooks and crannies. Pointing. Sloppily. A street name. A house where so-and-so once lived. A Spanish cat. There. Look. Weird head. Long ears. He wanted to share it. This was his purpose in life. To be British and to share what he knew.

The beer made him see.

'Come on,' said Larry. He had sandals on. They slapped at the street. They almost made him trip. But not all the way. He waved his arm while he faced ahead. His arm in the air. A big sweep. 'This way, troops. Blood and battle.'

Ruth took his arm. He looked behind. Larry's wife was there. Dark. Drifting. Like a shadow. She watched him with her head tipped forward. Arms folded across her chest. She might have been facing the ground but her eyes were tilted up. It looked like she hated what she saw. Him.

He looked at Ruth. She smiled. Shook her head a little. Gave his arm a squeeze. He heard a hissing sound behind him. It was coming from Larry's wife. What the fuck was up with her?

They should get away.

'This is the late-night bar.' Larry kept walking. There didn't seem to be a bar in sight. 'This is it.' They walked more and more. Larry waving. Around a corner. Arm sweeping the air. Sandals slapping the pavement. Grunts coming out of him. The wife hissing behind. There were a few Spaniards. Older men stood near doorways. Black button-up sweaters. Black pants. Distinguished. Unhappy with what was passing in front of them. The display. A woman in a window. A black shawl over her head. Black dress. She had nothing in her face. When she watched them go by. Grey hair. Wrinkled lips muttering. A proper curse. A prayer.

He didn't like the feel of it.

'The late-night bar. It's here. Here. Look. I kid you not.'

A young Spaniard kept his eyes on Larry. The man was sitting on a scooter. He watched Larry go by and kept watching. A headful of thoughts about belonging.

Larry took another corner.

'This is it.' His voice coming from out of sight. Far away almost.

They went around the corner. Larry stood there. Clapping his pink hands together. Lifting them up like he couldn't believe the miracle of it. Shaking his joined hands above his head. The winner. 'Oh, I told you it was here. Didn't I say such?'

Music was playing through a doorway. Larry turned that way and stumbled into the bar. Calling out: '*Hola. Hola.*' Everyone his best friend. In the entire world. No matter what they thought.

He never danced. He didn't like to dance. But he danced that night. Danced with his new heart. The idea of how he might look. It came into his mind. He shut it down. What didn't matter now. He knew no one here. Except Ruth. When he woke. He remembered. Ruth was still sleeping. What was there to regret? That taste in his mouth. Scared again of himself. Nerves prickling under his skin. He went out on the balcony. There was only a little light. Two voices down in the tennis court. Waiting for the sun. Memories coming one at a time. Then together. Stopping. A few more. The music had been guitars. It wasn't a tape like he thought. When he was outside. About to go in. Men playing guitars. Singing words he did not understand. There was something to that. Their voices together. Almost stabbing at the guitars. Fast. Banging their guitars with their flat hands. Stomping their feet. Shoe leather snapping against wood. Working toward fury. Something he liked. It made him content. The stomping of those feet. To drink more. Larry shouting in his ear: They play guitars until their fingers bleed. This was a tip. Larry winked. With one side of his mouth open.

Women dancing. Hands over their heads. Men dancing with men. Arm in arm in circles. Two men dressed up like women. No one cared. Men with women. Women with women. It didn't matter. Everyone was dancing. Celebrating. They got him on his feet and made him dance. Larry first. Come on. Then Ruth. Smiling. She was smiling to see him this way. He didn't mind. The music was good for it. Larry's wife with her eyes. No food in her. Just brandy. Another. And another. When he went to the washroom that time. She was in there. Waiting. It was like he'd followed her. But he hadn't seen her. He thought about it. Had he seen her? She pushed him into a stall. Hissing. Snarling to show her teeth. She had her hand down his pants. Before he knew it. Against him. Pushing. He shoved her back. Not certain.

The music came louder. Someone opening the bathroom door. There were voices outside the stall. Foreign and fast. Leaning toward laughter. Two men. Talking while they pissed.

She just stayed there. Quiet. Waiting. Until they were gone. Music turning louder. Conversation rising. Then all of it blocked again.

'I know who you are,' she said. He wondered what she meant. She was from England. How would she know him? Looking in her eyes. He knew she was talking about something else. 'Worthless.' She pulled up her blouse.

Showed him. Squeezed herself. Like meat. Like a toy. The music outside. Wilder. Took his hand. Slapped it against her skin. Made his hand squeeze. 'With your pretty woman.' Laughed with her mouth open. Ugly. She came at him. With the same savagery. A switch flicked. Grabbing. Smacked him back against the stall. The noise for anyone to hear. The noise she was making. Her mouth wet and big on him. Hungry sounds. Her fingernails digging in. Down his pants. He shoved her back. She smacked the stall. Hit her head. She stared at him. Scared. She was scared. Scared of him. Scared of the world. Scared of herself. Then it went away. Something came over her. How she could change it. Shape it. He knew her too. He didn't know her. But he knew her. This was about where she came from. Not who she was. What she was. Where she came from. Not the place. Trying to be grand. Brutal under her clothes. Naked and brutal. The perfect way she pretended. Pretending through her life. Like him. And she lifted her skirt. No underwear. For when she did this. How often? With how many? Just waiting. Ready. She took his hand and forced it between her legs. Knees wide apart. Rubbed his palm back and forth. Too hard to be good.

Music and conversation. All louder again. The door opening. Shutting. No sound outside the stall. Maybe just one man.

This time, she didn't care.

'Yeah,' she said. Spitting. 'Like that.' She kissed him. Yanked him near. Both hands on his cheeks. Her body begging. His fingers were in her. One. Then three. Easily. 'Yeah.' Showing her teeth. 'Shove it.' The sneer. Like in a mirror. 'In me.' Her whole body struggling. But not with him. 'You like that.' Her eyes on him. 'Pig.' Her body moving faster. Rocking against him. Her eyes never shutting. Angry. Afraid. He was inside her. The thrust of his shoulder. Deeper inside. Making her worse. Making her stronger. She took his arm. 'No, no. Uh-uh. Bad boy.' Pulled it away. Out. She turned and left. The door to the stall open. He was breathing hard. No one there. He wiped his mouth. The stink off her. He waited. Wondering why. He washed his hands. Excited. For the first time in years.

When he came back out. Ruth there looking right at him. The bathroom door. The dancing. Larry's wife gone. But Larry still there. Wobbling. A drink in each hand. Afloat. He didn't even know. He had no idea. But Ruth was watching him. Ruth knew.

'See what dancing leads to,' he said.

It hurt when Ruth smiled. He could see that. Hurt her. And him. The harm done. What Larry's wife might have said to her. Just to ruin things. To put him in his place. It would take a while to get over it.

'How's your head?' he asked. He felt he had to talk. To see if she was hung-over. Or angry with him. To see how much she knew. Whose fault. To see how she felt about him. If it had changed. If last night mattered.

'Shhh.' She held up a hand and went into the bathroom. Shut the door. Locked it.

The car passed through a hilly desert. There had been orange trees. He could see the trees. They looked unwell. Like they were nothing but dying twisted branches. No leaves. But then the dots of orange. Or the dots of yellow. Lemon trees. Everything crystal clear at a distance. Unreal. Even the sunlight different here. Then desert. A town far off to the left. Like the Wild West. A wooden cowboy town. There by itself. Two sides of a street. That was all. Sitting in the middle of nowhere. Not a soul around. Not a single gunfight. No one mad enough to greet them with a warning.

'They must shoot movies there,' Ruth said. Her voice flat. Matter-of-fact. She was driving. Her only part in it. He didn't want to drive. He couldn't handle it. Not knowing where to go.

The town was gone. He imagined the rooms in those houses. Real rooms or just boxes of nothing.

They started climbing higher. The road moving out of desert. Through a small town. Signs of poverty. It looked like Mexico. Pictures he had seen. Or movies. A woman in a poncho. A straw hat. A few children who looked apart from everything. Struck dumb. Because of their car. Watching them pass through. A brown dog. Struck dumb too. Then land. Trees. Towns off in the distance. A clump of houses. Newer towns. Like they were made in a factory. All the same. Assembled. Not like the old white villages. Shaped every which way.

'Franco built those towns,' Ruth said.

He looked at her face. Who was Franco? What was he to her?

'So people had somewhere to live. But there's nothing to do.' She looked at him for a second. That was all. Like she was starting to forgive him. She had said nothing about blame. No fight. She kept it all to herself. Bottled up. 'I read about them. People just live there. They don't work. There's no work. They're like ghost towns.'

He watched the town. People lived there. But there was no movement. The streets empty. The town gone. More desert. Then another town. Just like the last one. The road going up. Climbing. Winding in a way you could barely feel. Not many cars on the road. Then a small old town with houses on both sides of the road. Not white. But brown and different. Low buildings. Most of them old. It had a feel to it. A proper town. Rooted. He knew he would like it there. They parked. It was almost night.

Stillness closing in. They needed to stop. Find a place to sleep. Getting out of the car. He knew they were up high. Maybe on a mountain. They had climbed for a while. He couldn't see down to know he was up high. It was all too gradual.

They rented a room. The old man at the counter didn't speak a word of English. Ruth spoke Spanish to him. The old man treated her like she was his long-lost daughter. Like he adored her. Like she was a princess. His old eyes watching her. Sacred. Wishing.

The room was small. They put their bags in there and left right away. Ruth wanted to explore. They went out walking around. Peaceful. Most of the people they passed lived there. Not like near the beach. Where everyone was from somewhere else. Wanting the way things were back home. He liked this better. Spain. The actual country. Then there was a castle wall. Right in the middle of the town. Like he had seen in the poster. In the travel-office window downtown. A castle or a fortress. That's what Ruth said: A fortress. An old brown wall. To protect the village. To keep everyone in. To keep the intruders out. Pale brown. Like sand. A bit of red in it. Just one wall. Trees next to it. Benches to sit on. Night shadows from leaves on the stones. They sat for a while. Watched the old men and women come by. The children run through. All dark-skinned. Dark suits. Blue sweaters. Dark dresses.

Shawls. Other younger women and men. In fashionable clothes. Done up perfect. Dresses with jewelry. Modest though. White shirts without a wrinkle. Creased black pants. A sweater maybe. V-neck pullover. Navy blue. Or red. They smoked cigarettes everywhere. One hand in the pocket. The other holding a cigar-ette. Smoking. Looking from one place to another. Younger couples sitting. In each other's arms. Kissing like that was the only thing that ever mattered. Sitting on a bench and kissing for minutes at a time. Arms around each other. Lovers. Nothing else existed.

The rabbit they ate was killed and skinned out back that day. The vegetables were from the owner's garden. The clay washed off. The peel still on. It was like a stew. It was just what he needed. Like eating in someone's home. Welcome. Have what I have. What I own. Take it. I insist. The owner wanted to please. That was his life. Big rough hands from working. He laid the plates down himself. It wasn't easy. What he did. Soil and animals. It made him happy to know. They were enjoying what he had given them. He stood by the table. Arms behind his back. Bent slightly forward. And watched. Not too long. Nodding. Smiling. Then he left them to each other.

'You like this?' Ruth asked.

'Yeah.'

She waited. Ate a bite. Chewed quietly. 'Not just the food.'

'I know.' He felt that it was time. Time that it was said. Before he felt it come on. The tension. Lockdown. But he wouldn't look at her. His eyes on his food. 'I'm sorry.'

Another stretch of silence. 'There're vipers everywhere. It's not your fault.' She said his name.

Her voice made him look. There was candlelight on her skin. In her eyes. A small fire lit in the corner. A comfortable heat. Light touching her hair in places. She was like a painting. Still. She sat still and watched him for a while. While he kept his eyes on her face.

'What?' she finally said.

'You know.' He was feeling something more for her. It was joyous. Joyous. That was the word.

They went for another walk after dessert. Something called flan. Pudding in caramel sauce. It was like the perfect dessert. He wanted to take as much of it as possible. Home with him. Where could he get some? Ruth said she could make it. Anytime he wanted. It wasn't that difficult.

A slow walk. No hurry. Because they had eaten now. They were full. They barely spoke. They went into a café where two old men were sipping coffee. Little white cups on saucers. At a small table with each other. One of them was talking. Explaining something. Carefully. The old man's hand patiently out. Speaking patient words. The old man's voice rough. The bartender was friendly. Both hands on the bar. Ready to help. A huge leg of meat hung to one side. Behind the bar. Tied up by a hoof. It caught his eye. The flies he noticed next. Swirling out into the air. Landing back on the meat. One of the old men pointed at the leg. The bartender nodded. He opened two bottles of lemon drink for them. He used a bottle opener. Old-fashioned. The bottle caps falling into a slot. On top of others.

'*Caz limón*,' Ruth had said. '*Dos*.' Two fingers held up.

The bartender didn't ask for money right away. He smiled and turned to slice a piece of meat from the leg. A big sharp knife. Easily cutting. Another slice. He didn't mind the flies. He laid the slices neatly on a big white plate. A real one. Not styrofoam.

Ruth drank from the glass bottle. They stood at the bar and then Ruth looked over her shoulder. Moved to a small table she saw. Little blue tiles on the top of it. People came and went away again. They were visiting. They came by every night. It seemed that way. They were all from here. They spoke loudly. Argued it seemed. But nothing came of it. Loud talk that was almost playful. More bottles opened. Glasses of wine poured. Coffees in little white cups. More meat cut from the bone. No one seemed to mind the flies at all. He wondered how long the meat had been hanging there. It scared no one in the room. Except him.

Back at the hostel. Upstairs. Ruth sat on the edge of the bed. She seemed shy. All of a sudden. Gone shy. What was in her mind? He came out of the bathroom. Listening to the strange toilet flush. She was sitting there. Hands on her knees. She kicked off her sandals. One at a time. The new ones she had bought from outside a shop. Newspapers for sale there too. From all over the world. The ocean across the street. Back at that town where so much was meant to be bought. The sea. He was used to the ocean. The Atlantic. This was a sea. The Mediterranean. It was hard to wear anything else in this heat. Never was much for shorts. But it was necessary here.

He stood still. Waiting for her to speak. He thought something might be the matter. He was always expecting it. Things to be over. People realizing. How wrong things were. How actually wrong. What was inside him. Really. Ruined. The danger of him. Doreen Stagg. Shut it down. No one ever knew. How much he was trying. People kept changing. What was needed to keep things straight? To fit together forever. Things to be over. Finally.

He went to the window. Opened the wooden shutters. He could see right down into the street. Small cars parked there. Yellow. White. Red. People still walking around. Quietly. The night a part of everything down there. Nothing to be afraid of. Nothing to escape. It was just life. Darkness. Why was that different here?

'How long are we staying?' She'd turned her head to look at him. Her voice came clearer when she said his name. Still on the bed.

He shifted to face her. 'You want to go home?' Always a reaction.

'No.'

He leaned back against the wall.

'Why don't you ever touch me?' She said it right away. Then she said his name again. Two different things. What she meant and then his name. Like it mattered. Those letters. That word. His first name. He hated it. His father's name too. Given to him by his father. To make certain.

Mister Myrden.

He cleared his throat. Looked toward the window. This place they had flown to. An experience that had nothing to do with life. Like he knew it. Life. Then he looked back at her.

'It's okay. But, you know.' She smiled. Hinting at something. Almost embarrassed. Her sweet voice. 'I'd like you to.' She was like a young woman. A teenager. It ripped at his heart. I'd like you to.

He didn't know what to say. Nothing was any good for him. Nothing excited him. How did he explain it? Then he thought of Larry's wife. Lawrence's wife. He didn't remember her name. Larry said it once at dinner. Introductions not important. She had done something for him. What was it? It was ugly. It was awful. What she thought of him. What she knew. Not what could be saved. What could be taken. What he deserved. Punishment. Greed. There was no difference between them. Punishment and greed. Plugged black in the mouth. He could have bitten right through her. That would have fixed him. Ruth wasn't like that. How could she know?

He looked at her. He loved her. He couldn't love her enough.

'Is there something the matter?'

He sighed. Folded his arms.

'With me,' she added.

'Ruth?'

'Yes?'

He didn't answer. He wondered who she was named after. What she was like as a girl. Who were her friends then? Where was her house? She watched him. She stood and went into the bathroom. This he took to mean crying. He listened. His body expecting that sound. Locked in the bathroom. A safe place. Crying. After the hurt. You're not hurt. You'd know it if you were hurt. But she came out in a while. Dry-eyed. In just her underthings. Baby-blue panties. Baby-blue bra. Her hair pinned up at the back. She walked over to him. Kissed him. Just the kiss. Her lips. Slow on his. Gently pressed there with meaning.

He looked at her eyes.

'I love you,' she said. The kiss had done that.

He couldn't help staring at her eyes. How they drew the words out of him. 'I love you,' he said. But it wasn't any good. Was it? What it did to him. Nearly wrecked him. But it was good. He had to tell himself. It was honest. Convince himself. 'I love you, Ruth.'

Her wet eyes. Her lips seeming fuller. Warmer when she kissed him again. Just the kiss. The way she meant it. Her hands on his face. Her tears against his cheeks. He could feel the flow of them. Hers and his.

That kiss. It was enough. It was almost enough. The harmless rising in his chest.

'I'm ovulating,' she said. In a voice as small as what she was thinking.

Chapter Seven

He had a feeling in the airport. He was lighter. It was good to be home. With Ruth. They had held hands on the airplane. Most of the way over. Things had changed. They definitely had. He and Ruth together in every sense. A vacation. He had heard how going away could help. Take your mind off your troubles. Give you perspective. He knew that word. He liked it. The more he said it in his mind. Perspective. There were plans in his head now. Plans he could see with everything in perspective. He was going to set up trust funds for his children. Like the lawyer had suggested. For Caroline. Even the boys. Try to make amends. Then maybe travel again with Ruth. He wanted to be with her. Heading home. He wanted to leave again. Right away. What would happen with his wife? He would have to split everything. Leave it to his lawyer. Stay out of it. His wife wouldn't know what to do with the money. It'd be gone and she'd be looking for more. He'd have to invest it. Like the lawyer said. All in time. He saw how it would be. There was no question. Always something to deal with. The years running on. Tangling.

The air was sweet outside the airport. Spruce trees at the edge of the parking lot. Cold. He wasn't expecting it. Didn't have on a coat. The chill cut through him. His skin still smelled of Spain. The taxi drivers spoke in a way he recognized. People he had seen all his life. Faces born there.

They got a taxi to her house. He had presents for Jackie and Caroline. Lots of little souvenirs in his suitcase. From here and there. A story to every one of them. Where each one was bought. A small village. A seaside resort. A religious shrine on a hill. Photographs of the different places. He couldn't wait to get the film developed. Doubles. A set for him. A set for Ruth. To show Jackie and Caroline. He called their house. The new number. The house he had bought for them. The house they had agreed to live in. Anxious to talk. To tell Jackie what it was like. She would appreciate it. What he was feeling. She would understand. There was no answer. He looked at the clock in Ruth's kitchen. 4:15 p.m. What time was it in Spain? It all came back to him. Vivid. The white houses. The beach. The castle wall. A fortress. The leg of meat. Larry. Larry's wife. Who do you think you are? And Ruth on that hostel bed. Bits of memories he would go through for years to come.

He heard a sigh from Ruth and saw her in the living room. Threw herself on the couch. 'Tired,' she said when he came in.

He was in her house. This he noticed. He was back there. Where did this house come from? It was someone else's. Like his wife's. Maybe Ruth would let him pay for half of it. Would that make it better?

'When do you have to work?'

'Monday morning.'

He thought through the days of the week. It was Thursday. What would they do until then? He wanted to move around. To explore like they had done in Spain. Find places he hadn't seen before. There didn't seem any point. To standing still.

Later. He called the number again. There was no answer. 5:10 p.m. Maybe they were out for supper. He worried a little. He'd been away. There was always the worry of bad things. It was with him. Sat with him. Slept with him. It came up big and black in his head. The slightest suspicion. The fingerings of dread. Something must go wrong. No. He shut it off. Shut it down. Stopped himself. But it came back.

'What's the matter?'

He sat next to her on the couch. Looked at the piano. The suitcases next to it. Unpacked. Let's go, he said in his head. Let's go, now. Quick. Let's hurry out of here. Let's get a plane.

'Nothing.'

'You're not saying much.'

'I was calling Caroline.'

'No answer.'

'No.'

In a while she got up. Cooked dinner. 6:35 p.m. He called the number again. His heart knew something. Smothered panic. Fear fit his body. He'd been away for two weeks. Those were the two weeks when anything might happen. When he was away. It would be his fault then.

'Food,' Ruth called out.

He ate a little. He wasn't hungry. His stomach was burning. Sour and bitter in his mouth. Ruth with her eyes on him. Knowing something bad would happen. Not might happen. But would. She always knew. Like when they were together first. Wasn't that why he left her? He remembered now. One of the reasons. That look. He could do with a beer. But it wouldn't do any good now. One beer. Twenty beers. He looked at the telephone. His arm hurt. Went weak. Then a little numb. He squeezed his hand into a fist. Held it that way. He wondered if it was just fear. Or this place. This house.

7:10 p.m. He called again.

'Why don't you go by?' Ruth knew. She knew.

He was contagious.

A thought struck him. He got up and called his wife's number. His wife answered. He could barely hear her. It was full of static.

'Where you been?' she asked. His fault.

'Is Jackie there?'

'No. Where you been?'

'Toronto,' he said. That was all he would say. It was the truth.

'What for?'

'How's Caroline?'

'I had to keep checking the money.' This said with a strange laugh. Like someone was with her. The laugh for someone else. Her voice crackling. 'Thought you ran . . .'

Her voice was lost for a while. Then it came back, 'I'm on my cellphone. Got the number put through. I'm in my new car. A Cadillac. Got a driver. On Slattery Street. By the supermarket. Going to bingo.'

'I was calling Jackie's house.'

'Wha'? You're breaking up. Hell—'

'I was calling Jackie's house.'

'The . . . new one?'

'Yeah.'

'I can hear ya now. Willis wrecked that one.'

'Wrecked what?'

'The new house.'

'Where are they?'

'Back in the old house. Nothing the matter with—'

He hung up. He wouldn't look at Ruth. She was near. She saw his face. He turned away. Dialed the old number. Jackie answered. She was tired. He could tell. Tired at 7:15 p.m. Worn out.

'Jackie.'

'Dad?' Worried. Why? Because he was gone? Or for herself?

'What're you doing?'

'Where are you?'

'Here.'

'You okay?'

'Okay? Sure. How's Caroline?'

There was a moment. Not a good one. 'Fine.'

'What's the matter?'

'Nothing.' Her wet voice. A teary bubble in her throat.

'Let me talk to Caroline.'

There was silence. A hand over the receiver. The angry voice of a man, muffled: 'Who's that?' He could hear it through the hand that tried to cover it over.

'It's Poppy.'

'Hello?'

'Caroline.'

'Hi.' She was sad.

'How are you?'

'Okay.'

'I bought you a present.'

'From where?' A bit of excitement. But not like her. Not enough of herself.

'I was on a trip.'

A roar from the man's voice.

'Okay. I got to go now.'

'Hello?'

Jackie back on. 'I'll see you.' She hung up.

He waited. He stood there. He breathed out all the breath he had. His head ached. His jaw ached. He watched the floor. It was a while before he breathed again. He hung up. He looked at Ruth. Her eyes changed when she saw what was in his face.

Ruth drove him to the house. She was talking. She was telling him things that were meant to hold him back. He never said a word. Along the way. All the space before his eyes. Just staring. The space pressing in on him. More and more as they went ahead. Piling up on him. The streets. The houses. The trail back to there.

The car stopped.

'Don't wait,' he said.

'What're you doing? What's–'

'Go on.' He got out of Ruth's car. That's one of the

things they had taught him about inside. Ownership. Respect other people's property. Other people's lives. No one has the right. People who have worked hard for what they have. Ruth's car. He got out of it. Ruth should drive away in her car. She should take what was hers and leave. Take what was his.

In front of him. The door. Willis's house. He turned to see Ruth still parked there. She drove ahead a bit. Stopped. Turned her head. Leaned a little to stare at him. Don't.

He opened the door to Willis's house and went in.

Calm down. Calm.

'Hello?'

Jackie came out of the kitchen. Wondering who it was. What might happen. Both eyes black. Black and sacred purple. Speckles of bright red. Her hand to her mouth. Her lips. Her fingers there. Just touching. Checking her lips. One arm in a sling.

'Dad?' Her voice broken up.

He stood next to her. A holiday. Tears spilling down his cheeks. A fucking holiday in the fucking sun. His tanned fists.

'Where's Caroline?' He did not know what to expect. He did not want to see. He did not want to know. He thought he might slap his hands over his ears. He did it. He shouted. He kept his hands there. He roared. His knees buckled. He came apart. He came apart. Piece by piece. He came apart. The house shook. Every wall. Every window. Every glass in the cupboards. Every plate. Things tipped over in the house. Things broke in half. He turned with his mouth open. His eyes open. He snorted. Took his hands from his ears. He snorted ahead. Up into the kitchen at the back. No one.

'Caroline?'

In the living room. She was on the couch. Told to sit there. Told not to move. A bruise on her face. One eye swollen shut. Hands tucked between her knees. Tears blurring everything out of sight. He rushed to her. Picked her up in his arms. Held her. One hand on her hair. On the back of her head.

You're not hurt.

'Poppy.' Her voice so small. She weighed practically nothing. Light as a feather. Just a little girl. He carried her out to where Jackie was in the hallway. Her feet bouncing in mid-air.

'Where is he?'

Jackie shook her head. Her eyes flinching. Upstairs. She couldn't help but give it away. Her eyes flinching toward upstairs. Toward the sound of the bathroom door closing. Locking. He went past Jackie. Reached for the front door. Opened it. Stood Caroline on her feet. On the curb.

Safe now.

'I love you,' he said to her. Bent down. Watching her face. Trying to remember. Her unmarked skin. The purity. How it used to be. The difference there now. The blackness. The seep. His teeth grinding together. He didn't know what his face looked like. He couldn't help it. He said it again. Tried to make it better. So she would see. He wasn't all bad.

Big wet tears in Caroline's eyes. Nodding. Fat tears spilling. 'I know, Poppy.'

'You're the only thing I ever loved in this world.'

Jackie there behind him. Coming slow. Walking slow because it hurt. She stopped there in the doorway. Watched back. Didn't know if she should leave. Didn't know if she should go. Could go. Could step out of that house.

Get out.

Ruth's car backing up. The sound of reverse. It stopped right next to him. Ruth's car. Ruth's life. He opened the back door.

'Get in.' He put Caroline in there. She was shivering. On the seat without a coat. Safe. Protected. 'Turn up the heat.'

Jackie still in the doorway. Staring out. Staring at him. Staring down at the concrete step. Staring back in. Her good hand coming up. Reaching out for Caroline. Her

-280-

face a mess of not knowing. Lost. Adrift. Maybe it was like that. Or maybe she wanted his help.

He went to her. Took her arm. Trembling. Her trembling. Him trembling. Two of their bodies like that. Barely bodies at all. Coming out of themselves. Trouble stepping down the concrete stairs. Trouble walking toward the car. Trouble bending down. Trouble getting in.

'Take them,' he said to Ruth. She nodded right away. Shook her head. Who did this? Tears in her eyes too. She saw what was happening. What had been done. 'Drive.' He slammed shut the door. Hard.

Caroline's eyes on him through the window. Trapped. Her eyes saying: Who are you? What is this? I'll never understand.

Jackie watching ahead. Ashamed. Shame. Guilt.

Ruth. His name from her mouth behind glass. Barely in his ears. The moment of conception.

Shut it down.

Ruth had felt it, she said. The exact moment of conception. When they were together in bed. Five nights ago in a foreign country.

Shut it off.

She had told him in the car. On the way over here. To this place. The time to let him know.

'Go,' he yelled. So she'd turn her eyes away. So she would not see.

And the car rolled forward.

He looked at the open door to Willis's house. He checked to see the car was far enough gone. Slowly rolling more. No one knowing what to do. At the stop sign up ahead. A second later. Around the corner. Three female faces turned to see. A memory of him. A good memory of him. Please.

Then he went back inside.